THE SUCCUBUS
SINS OF THE FLESH

A Novel By

VANNA B.

HOPE
STREET
publishing

ISBN: 978-0-9853515-3-3

Cover model: Lola Von Bomb
Make-up & hair: Rosemary Ashley
Photography & cover design: RJ Jacques.

Hope Street Publishing
P.O. Box 2705
Philadelphia, PA 19120

Acknowledgements

Thank you Lord for your continued blessings. I could ask no more of you than what you've already done for me. Thank you for allowing me to find so much inspiration in the world around me and for allowing me to constantly hone and perfect the creativity you've given me.

Mom and Dad, you guys should not be reading this book but if you've gone against my warnings and picked it up anyway, just be prepared for the X-rated content within it! LOL. Thank you for creating me and loving me. I love you both.

Thank you to my husband, Akbar, and my entire family for continuing to support my dream.

Thank you to all my readers who embraced this endeavor into a genre that is completely new to me. Your open-mindedness and acceptance of *The Succubus* really shows me just how many true supporters I have and I couldn't be happier.

Thank you to all my true friends who are constant supporters and genuinely happy for me.

Quiana J., thank you for all of your advice and wisdom. As a fellow author/publisher that puts great effort into constantly learning, growing, and outdoing yourself, I have tremendous respect for you and am glad to call you a friend.

Qiana D., thank you for taking the time to read my projects in advance and for providing your input. You always have my back and you are someone that I can honestly say is a true lover of literature. You wear many hats and I admire the passion and pride with which you do all that you do.

Lola, thank you for bringing my vision of Raven to life in an awesome way. And thank you, Rosemary, for also being a part of it.

Thank you from the bottom of my heart to all of you that are readers and supporters of my work. Please keep providing your honest feedback and I will continue to write books that you love!

Sincerely,

Vanna

Chapter One

"So lemme get this straight," a muscled, tanned student blurted out, rising from his seat in his Comparative Mythology class to gain everyone's attention. "You mean to tell me this demonic woman, Huldra, would run through the forest naked, seducing random men? Sounds like my type of girl!" The class erupted into a boisterous bout of laughter.

From the back of the huge lecture hall Darrin Brown shook his head at the young man's crude comment, noticing that the name displayed on the back of his Columbia University Lions football jersey read "B. Rick." *Fitting name*, Darrin mused, *especially considering he's dumb as a brick*. Amused with his witty observation, his chuckle blended in with the rest of his classmates' laughs.

"Okay, okay…that's enough!" Professor Hubert demanded, reclaiming control of his class. "Huldra is the most widely known succubus in Norwegian folklore; very similar to Qarinah in Arabian mythology and Mohini of India. Now can anyone tell me the name of the most popular succubus in Christianity? I'll give you a hint. She was said to be Adam's first wife."

Darrin quickly raised his hand, sure that he undoubtedly knew the answer.

"Yes, Mr. Brown?"

"It's Eve," he stated with confidence.

"Incorrect," Professor Hubert said, shooting down his response.

Confused, Darrin replied, "Everyone knows Eve was Adams wife."

"Actually," a girl dressed in dark, gothic attire, said from several rows in front of him, "Lilith was Adam's first wife. Eve was merely created as an afterthought because Lilith was too strong-willed for Adam. Lilith refused to lie down and be submissive, so she was cursed and turned into a succubus as punishment."

"That can't be right," laughed Darrin. "I was brought up in the church and I've never once heard that story."

"Then it appears you've been misled," she fired back at him, never breaking her stony-eyed gaze.

Darrin opened his mouth to respond, but was interrupted by Professor Hubert's speech.

"Actually, what Ms. DuBois said is correct. Lilith was turned into a succubus and began carrying out her revenge by seducing and killing men. And because she never ate the forbidden fruit as Adam and Eve did, she was untainted by the original sin, and thus unable to die. She was said to be immortal and was considered a demon. Afterwards, God created Eve from Adam's rib, and since she was made from a piece of him instead of from the earth as Adam was, she was more subservient – a perfect woman."

"A perfect woman?" the oddly dressed young Ms. DuBois interjected, her face twisting into a disapproving scowl. "That's your idea of a perfect woman?" she scoffed, rolling her eyes at the preposterous claim. "A real woman won't allow a man to control her, because she knows that men are weak, feeble-minded creatures. Women are naturally more intelligent and capable. Lilith was the perfect woman."

"Lilith was certainly a headstrong woman. No argument there," someone stated in response. Raven shot a warning look at the blonde-haired beauty, staring into her icy blue eyes threateningly as she spoke. "But you've failed to mention the fact that Lilith was also an evil demon bitch who murdered innocent infants."

"You better learn to watch your tongue," Raven hissed at her classmate.

"Yes Aria, no profanity in class, please," Professor Hubert said. "You're absolutely right, though; succubi were said to have killed babies and children out of jealousy or spite."

The professor glanced at his watch and bid his class farewell, prompting Darrin and the other students to close their books and begin filing out of the auditorium. As he exited the building, Darrin noticed the goth girl walking in his direction, giving him the opportunity to get a good look at her for the first time.

With her dark make-up and long, bright red hair, she certainly wasn't your conventional girl next door. She donned black leather pants with seemingly useless zippers all over them, a red and black lace brocade corset, and fishnet arm warmers that allowed her sleeve tattoos to remain visible from beneath the tight netting. Her platform knee boots added an extra six inches to her mere 5'4" stature, and dozens of heavy gunmetal chains dangled from her wrists and neck, jingling as she made her way closer to Darrin. But despite her odd manner of dress, he could not ignore her obvious beauty. Her brown skin was smooth and radiant, and her heart-shaped lips, full and succulent. They were painted a deep red – the shade of dried blood – and her bottom lip bore a small silver hoop piercing that connected to her nose ring by a thin chain, while her left eyebrow was adorned with a single stainless steel barbell. Along with the layers of chains, a lone jewel hung around her neck. To the average observer, it appeared to be just a pretty stone – onyx or a black sapphire perhaps. But to Raven, the amulet was much more. She sucked on a cigarette, staining its tip with the dark cherry gloss from her lips.

"Hey, Jesus freak," she said, peering into his deep brown eyes through the lenses of his thick spectacles. "Sorry to burst your bubble about the Eve thing." She took a drag from her cigarette, allowing the smoke to waft slowly from her nostrils, curling into ribbons in the air before vanishing into the atmosphere.

"Um…uh…yeah, it's okay," Darrin bumbled nervously, his eyes quickly dropping to ground to avoid making eye contact with her. "That's what I'm here for – to learn new things."

He shyly raised his eyes from the floor, but the gaze intended for her flawless-complexioned face instead fell upon the perky D-cup breasts being squeezed up and out of her tight corset. He quickly dropped his eyes back to the ground.

"Yeah, well…see ya' around," she said before turning on her heels and strutting off.

Darrin watched his mysterious classmate cross Amsterdam Avenue and disappear into a thick crowd of bustling New York pedestrians before continuing on to his next class.

VANNA B.

Chapter Two

Darrin's following class, Political Science, was one that he looked forward to attending every Monday, Wednesday, and Friday, not so much due to the subject matter, but because it was the only class that he and his girlfriend, Melody, had together. He spotted the light of his life sitting at a desk near the windows and was preparing to take the open seat next to her when a push from behind sent him flying forward, causing him to trip over a desk leg and fall face flat onto the floor. His glasses landed in front of him and he scrambled to pick them up, thankful that they were not broken.

"Sorry, loser. This seat's taken," said the tanned jock from his previous class as he slid into the chair next to Melody.

"Leave him alone, Brandon!" Melody yelled in her boyfriend's defense. "All these open seats in here and you have to steal his?"

"It's okay, Mel," Darrin said, diffusing the situation. Not one to engage in confrontation, he sulked away to find himself another seat.

Though Darrin had grown up in the roughest part of Detroit, one would've never known by looking at him. For as long as he could remember, his daily attire consisted of a collared shirt tucked into his high-water khakis or jeans that he'd iron a sharp crease into, just as his mother had taught him. Paired with brown loafers and his signature wire-framed bifocals, he was anything but cool. He lived an extremely sheltered life. His single mother loved him with all her heart and was very overprotective of her only child. From elementary through high school, Darrin was to go directly to the after-school program at their Baptist church as soon as school let out. Sports were out of the question as they were too dangerous, and playing outside in the street was unheard of. Darrin would often watch NFL games on TV and root for his home team, the Lions, then sit in his window and watch the neighborhood boys outside playing tackle football in the middle of the street. He longed to join them; he was sure he could play skillfully and impress them with his speed and strength if given the chance. But the only time Darrin was allowed outside was to go to school or to church.

Church wasn't all too bad though, thanks to Melody. Darrin and his slim, long-legged sweetheart had become friends 15 years ago when her family moved into the house across the street and began attending his church. In many ways Melody's life was somewhat similar to Darrin's. She, too, was raised by strict, religious parents and spent much of her time in the church, but she had not been nearly as sheltered as Darrin. She'd always thought Darrin was handsome and she liked that he was quiet and shy like her. In middle school, they had been each other's first kiss and first love. They both knew they would one day take each other's virginity, but not until they were married, of course.

Darrin and Melody were thrilled upon learning they were both accepted to Columbia University's School of Social Work and would not have to be away from each other. Darrin's mom pleaded with him not to leave; she begged him to stay home and attend Wayne State University in Detroit, selfishly asking him to forego an Ivy League education, but there was no way Darrin was going to continue to live as a prisoner confined to his mother's house. He was a grown man now and he had waited his whole life for the day he'd finally be able to step out into the world.

But not much had changed since Darrin and Melody's arrival in New York City. When he wasn't in class, he spent most of his time in his dormitory studying. Sometimes he'd sit in the library or the food court to people watch, but when he was not with Melody, he was by himself. Still painfully shy and a social outcast, Darrin didn't know how to make friends and he knew no one wanted to be friends with someone like him anyway. Darrin's roommate did his best to stay clear of him. And even Melody had been quite busy as of late. Unlike him, she had many friends, and although she wasn't big on partying, she stayed involved with numerous activities including the Horticulture Club, the Choral Arts Society, the Science Club, and volunteering at a nearby soup kitchen.

Melody abandoned her seat for the empty desk next to Darrin. He smiled as she approached him and planted a soft kiss on his cheek.

"Hey, you," she said, her light brown eyes twinkling as she flashed her pearly whites. "How's your day going?"

"Same ol', same ol'," he shrugged. "I miss you, Mel. You're always so busy these days. You think we could hang out tonight? Watch a movie or something?"

"Awww, I can't tonight, Darrin." She twirled a lock of her shoulder-length sandy brown hair around her slender index finger. "My roommate's in a play and she'll be absolutely crushed if I'm not there."

"Well maybe—"

"It's sold out," she cut him off, as if reading his mind, "and she only had one extra ticket for me."

"Okay then," he sighed, feeling defeated. "Maybe tomorrow."

Chapter Three

Two days later, Darrin sat alone in the cafeteria picking over the remainder of his tuna sandwich and watching the other students coast effortlessly through the day. He looked at his digital calculator watch, noticing he still had another half hour remaining until the start of Comparative Mythology class. He was startled from his trance when someone suddenly pulled out the metal chair across from him and plopped down in the seat. It was the weird gothic girl from his class.

"What's up, Jesus freak?" she asked, staring him directly in the face as she obnoxiously chewed and smacked on her pink bubblegum.

Darrin looked around nervously and swallowed hard. "Hello."

"Chill out, man," she said, stopping to blow and pop a huge bubble. "I don't bite…well, sometimes I do, but you look a little too bland for my taste. What's your name, anyway?"

"Darrin."

"I'm Raven," she said, sticking out her hand for him to shake. He inspected her fingerless maroon lace gloves and long, pointy black-lacquered fingernails apprehensively before shaking her hand.

"If you don't mind me asking," he hesitantly began, "why do you dress like that?"

"I was about to ask you the same damn thing!" Raven chuckled in response.

"Well...I...I," he stuttered, looking down at his faded green polo shirt and tan khakis, not finding anything the least bit unusual about his attire.

"I get it," said Raven. "You got your own style. I got my own, too. I refuse to be one of these sheep, walking around here following the fucking herd. Instead, I'm a wolf, scaring the shit out of them!" Raven raised her head to the ceiling and let out a loud, high-pitched howl, drawing several inquisitive glances.

Among the gawkers was Aria. Standing several feet from their table, she shook her head in disgust while giving Raven the evil eye.

"Fuck you lookin' at, bitch?" Raven spat at her, returning the hateful glare.

"Who me? I'm looking at nothing, because that's exactly what you are." Aria moved a loose strand of her thin, straight hair behind her ear, blending it in with the rest of her platinum blonde bob, folded her arms across her chest, and continued focusing her frigid gaze on Raven.

"What's with you two?" Darrin whispered to Raven.

"This bleach blonde bitch over here likes to act like she has an eye problem. But unless she wants more problems, I think it's in her best interest to FUCK OFF." Raven never took her eyes off Aria as she spoke; she didn't even blink.

"Now Raven," Aria smiled, "you and I both know your bark is much worse than your bite."

The spectators continued to watch the confrontation unfold. The exchange between the two women was much more entertaining than whatever was playing on the flat screen televisions mounted throughout the cafeteria. Annoyed by their nosiness, Raven decided to give them the show they wanted.

"BOO!" she yelled at the curious onlookers, slamming both hands on the table, startling them and causing them to quickly turn away and continue on about their business. The force made the wobbly table rock, and her red skull and crossbones pen rolled off the table and onto the floor.

"Could you get that for me, Darrin?" she cooed, batting her long black lashes.

Aria simply shook her head again and walked toward the door. *Poor Darrin*, she thought to herself as she exited the food court. *He has no idea what he's getting himself into.*

Darrin poked his head under the table and spotted the pen resting between Raven's paten-leather platform boots. Squatting down to all fours, he crawled over to retrieve it. As he inched closer to Raven, she spread her legs wide and Darrin experienced the burning temptation to look at what was between them. He quickly retrieved the pen, being careful to keep his eyes glued to the floor as he slowly backed away. But against his will, his gaze diverted back to her outrageous boots. *One, two, three, four,* his heartbeat quickened as he counted the metal buckles lined up the front of one boot. With a mind of their own, his eyes continued creeping up her leg to her torn fishnet thigh-high stockings, and he was unable to stop them from wandering all the way up to her crotch.

Darrin's eyes bulged in their sockets once he realized Raven wasn't wearing any panties. Her plump, shaven pussy sat completely exposed beneath the frilly layers of her black tutu, and a sparkling silver ring decorated her pierced clitoris. Darrin had never seen a woman's vagina up close before – only those in an issue of Playboy his roommate had showed him – but he couldn't help but notice that unlike the ones belonging to the magazine girls, Raven's was unbelievably wet, glistening with her own creamy secretion. He took a deep breath, attempting to regain his composure before coming up from under the table.

Without warning, Raven threw one of her legs around him, hooking his neck in the bend of her knee and pulling his face deep into the warm wetness between her thighs. Shocked, Darrin attempted to pull back, but his struggles to break free proved useless once she wrapped her other leg around him and began to squeeze tighter. Raven thrust her twat forward, rolling her hips and gyrating raunchily onto his face. His heart raced as the dangling ring was smashed against his nose. He breathed heavily, taking in her scent; it was an ambrosial mixture of melon and vanilla that caused Darrin's mouth to salivate. His lips were forced into her dripping wetness, getting a thorough coating of her honey-flavored juices. Raven's clit stiffened and her love hole contracted. Her juices oozed onto his lips as she continued to hump away at his face, using it as her own personal fuck toy.

Darrin couldn't believe what she was doing to him. His head jerked up and slammed into the table above. Still, his resistance was no match as Raven gripped the edge of the table and clenched her leg muscles tighter to keep him firmly locked in place while she continued to grind her love box onto his face.

"Mmmm," she moaned, enjoying the sensation without the slightest bit of regard for his desire to be released. Raven's legs tensed as she rolled harder. "Mmmmmmmm!" She bit down on her bottom lip, attempting to contain her moans of ecstasy as she gushed onto his face. Darrin was relieved when, at last, her taut leg muscles began to relax.

Finally she released him from the compromising leg lock, allowing him to come up for air. His head popped up form beneath the table and he struggled to catch his balance, almost falling out of his chair. Darrin threw the pen onto the table and began adjusting his crooked glasses. Raven grabbed her pen and strutted off, laughing uncontrollably, and leaving Darrin dumbfounded at

the table with a milky goatee and the hardest
erection   he'd   ever   had.

Chapter Four

Darrin could not deny his attraction to Raven. Despite all the dark make-up, intensely bright hair, and her strange manner of dressing, she was a gorgeous and alluring woman. The polar opposite of all that Darrin embodied, she was everything he wasn't: bold, sexy, defiant, and dangerous. Darrin knew she was trouble from the moment he laid eyes on her. But he'd never seen anyone like her before and that alone had him intrigued and curious to know more about her.

After their encounter in the food court, Darrin could not stop thinking about Raven. He attempted to block out the lustful images distracting him from his studies and preventing him from paying attention in class, but all throughout the day he'd find his mind wandering back to several days ago when his face was enclosed between the lovely, wet warmth of her spread legs. Each time he envisioned her beautiful genitalia, her intoxicating scent wafted into the air. He licked his lips and could taste the delectable remnants of her sweet essence. His mouth watered at the thought of tasting her again, and each time, he grew an instant erection and experienced much guilt as a result. He thought of Melody and recited the verse of Matthew 5:28 over and over again to himself: *I say unto you, that whosoever looketh on a woman to lust after her hath committed adultery with her already in his heart.* But Raven's non-stop groping and flirtation only made matters worse. Whenever she saw him, she was sure to taunt him with a quick flash of her goods or a firm grab to his crotch.

The next time he saw her was in the class in which he first became familiar with her – Comparative Mythology. He noticed her enter the room as he was taking his usual seat in the back row. He did his best to keep his gaze focused straight ahead and not look her way but she pranced right over to the row in which he was seated and headed directly toward him. He rose from his seat, allowing her ample space to pass him, but as she slid down the row she suddenly stopped, bending over right in front of him.

"Oops! Looks like my shoe came unbuckled," she sang in mock-innocence. "Let me fix it real quick." As she bent down pretending to fiddle with her shoe, she made sure to press her perfectly round rump right onto Darrin's package. Backed up against the folded seat as far as he could go, Darrin swallowed hard before glancing around to see if anyone noticed the sexual assault taking place. None of the few students in the room seemed to be paying them any mind as Raven pressed herself harder back onto Darrin, swaying her curvy hips methodically. His pipe rose to the occasion, straining against his already too-tight jeans.

Satisfied with his bulging hard-on, Raven let up, taking a seat beside him.

As Professor Hubert got set up in the front of the class to begin his lecture, Raven seductively ran her tongue along Darrin's neck, licking him from his collar bone to his earlobe, which she playfully nibbled, sucked, and flicked with her tongue ring. Darrin sat stiff as a board, nervously maintaining his forward stare.

When the professor turned to the class and began to speak, Raven whispered into Darrin's ear, "Pet my kitty." But Darrin refused to move. Raven began pulling on his hand and after a brief struggle he forfeited the game of tug of war and unstiffened his arm. Raven guided his hand beneath the shredded fabric of her charcoal gray skirt and helped his index and middle fingers find their way into her moisture. The smooth wetness of her pussy walls prompted his dick to harden even more. He wiped the sleeve of his free arm across his forehead to dry the beads of sweat that had formed as he mentally tried his best to relax and calm his jitters. As if working a puppet, Raven moved Darrin's wrist back and forth, using his fingers to pleasure herself. Moments later, Darrin felt a spurt of fluid onto his fingers and hand as she quietly climaxed. Once she released his hand he pulled it away, examining the warm, creamy glaze dripping down his wrist.

"Go on, Darrin," she urged, "Taste it." Darrin ignored her. He was pretending to be into what Professor Hubert was saying when Raven again prompted, "Taste it," this time lifting his hand up to his mouth. Darrin slowly parted his lips, swiping his tongue across a sticky fingertip before inserting it into his mouth. His taste buds tingled as they were reacquainted with Raven's honey-like flavor and his mouth instantly salivated for more of her delicious nectar. Darrin was unable to stop himself from sucking all of the sweet coating from both of his fingers. It was completely involuntary; somehow his body had managed to act without his brain's permission. He found himself licking the dripping juice from his hand and wrist, lapping up every drop like a starving cat would fresh spilled milk. When he finally noticed what he was doing, he froze and lowered his head in embarrassment.

With her hand under his chin, Raven lifted his head until they were eye-to-eye. She offered up one of her seductive smiles while easing her hand into his jeans to his still-erect member. Gripping it firmly, she began stroking up and down with skill. She was surprised at his size; he was long and thick for his stature – much bigger than she imagined. She worked the entire length of his shaft vigorously, devilishly smirking at every shudder that vibrated through his body. She enjoyed making him squirm. She felt a few drops of moisture escape the tip of his cock and used them as lubricant, increasing her speed and applying additional pressure to the swelling head of his thick penis. Darrin gripped the arm of the chair to stabilize himself as his body tensed up and he spasmed uncontrollably, unintentionally exploding inside of his pants.

"Shit!" he exclaimed, jumping up and startling the quiet of the class. Professor Hubert halted his lecture and all the students spun around, curious about the sudden profane outburst. Darrin was just as surprised by his exclamation as everyone else, and even more stunned that a four-letter word had escaped his lips.

"Uh, sorry," Darrin uttered, frantically gathering his belongings and using his jacket to block onlookers' vision of the large wet spot on the front of his jeans. Raven tried her hardest to stifle her laugh as she watched Darrin scurry out of the auditorium.

VANNA B.

Chapter Five

Despite feeling continued guilt over his lustful visions and acts, and trying his absolute hardest to dismiss any lecherous thoughts of Raven, Darrin continued to be plagued by his dirty daydreams. They remained a great distraction with sexual fantasies of her invading his thoughts day and night. Their sneaky public fiascos replayed in his head over and over and he reveled in their memory. Darrin began to find it necessary to masturbate several times a day while picturing Raven's nude, tattooed body lying in his bed. After all, he had eventually concluded, the real sin would be to walk around with all that pent-up sexual frustration inside of him; he simply had to release the pressure.

One night, while Darrin was alone in his dorm room doing homework, there was a knock at the door. Assuming it was someone looking for his roommate, he yelled through the door that John wasn't in at the moment. Seconds later, the knocking continued, so Darrin reluctantly pulled himself away from his assignment to answer the door. He swung it open and his jaw dropped in astonishment when Raven pushed him forcefully back inside the room.

Without speaking, she threw open her black velvet trench coat, revealing her incredible, curvaceous body. Allowing the coat to slide to the floor, she slowly and seductively walked toward him. Darrin could not believe his eyes as the woman of his daily fantasies and wet dreams stood before him, exposed. Aside from her red, six-inch stiletto pumps, sheer, black crotch-less stockings, and the black jewel amulet she always wore around her neck, she was naked as the day she was born. His eyes widened as he took in the sight of her. Beneath the layers of dark, peculiar clothing, Raven had been hiding the body of a goddess. At the center of her voluptuous breasts sat small, pierced chocolate nipples and her derrière was plump and round. Her hips boasted womanly curves accentuated by the thin waist she'd been cinching for years and had successfully trained down to a tiny 20-inch circumference. Aside from the tattoos covering both of her arms in their entirety, the only other ink gracing her body included a black rose on her right thigh and a raven within a flaming pentagram over her left breast with the words "vita aeterna" below it.

"W-w-what's that mean?" Darrin asked, pointing at the Latin phrase, his voice cracking as he trembled with apprehension.

"Eternal life," Raven replied, as she pushed him again, twice as hard as the first time. He stumbled backward and fell onto the bed. Raven immediately straddled him and began removing his clothing, piece by piece. The silver-toned crucifix hanging on the wall above Darrin's bed glimmered in the light streaming through the cracked blinds, catching her eye. Her beautiful face contorted into a disapproving scowl. After pulling his shirt over his head she tossed it at the cross, knocking it upside down – a position more to her liking. She smiled contently before averting her attention back to Darrin and the task of undressing the nervous virgin boy. Once she had successfully stripped him completely naked, she lowered her hips onto him and began sliding her wet slit all over his hardened shaft.

"Raven, I—"

"Shhhh." She placed a finger at his trembling lips, silencing him at once. "Just relax, Darrin. I know what I'm doing. I've been fucking long before you were even a sperm in your daddy's nut sack."

"Huh?" he asked, confused.

"I'm 220 years old, sweetie. I just look damn good for my age." Darrin could no longer hear what Raven was saying as her slick pussy lips continued to glide all over his erect penis, driving him wild. Finally, after toying with him for a while, she let the throbbing tip slip into her tight opening. She maintained control as she fucked the head without allowing him to fully penetrate her. Instead, she teased him for several more minutes, working the tip of his dick in and out, and winding her hips in small circles but still refusing to let the bulk of his member enter her orifice. Darrin was already on the verge of climaxing as Raven's cream dripped down his thick love pole to his testicles and had him eagerly anticipating the sensation of being deep inside of her. Her labia puckered as her vagina spasmed, hungrily tugging at his dick and drawing it in. At last, she gave in, sitting all the way down on his hard, waiting pipe. Darrin involuntarily let out a long, loud moan of pleasure at the delightful feeling of her narrow walls cradling his entire manhood. She grinded and rotated her hips in a rhythmic motion and to her surprise it wasn't long before she reached her peak.

"Ohhh, fuck!" she screamed out as she ejaculated, sending her nectar raining down onto his cock and balls. With her orgasm out of the way, Raven began bouncing up and down wildly on top of Darrin, her D-cup breasts jumping freely with each jerk. Smacking sounds resounded through the small room as their bodies forcefully met over and over again, causing the combination of sweat and sexual juices to splash about. Darrin's hands remained at his sides, gripping the sheets for stability as Raven bucked like a rodeo bronco. She grabbed his hands, placing them on her chest mounds before positioning herself up on her feet in a squatting position. Raven continued to ride him rough and hard, showing no mercy to his virginity. Darrin was lost in ecstasy and appeared possessed as his eyes rolled to the back of his head. She clenched her muscles tightly around his girth and

Darrin could no longer take it. He squeezed her breasts as if holding on for dear life and exploded deep inside her. Raven did not stop. She continued fucking him relentlessly, refusing to let up, even when he begged and pleaded. Darrin's convulsions gradually diminished as his sensitive penis slowly recuperated. Raven's pussy remained tight, and still saturated with her and Darrin's cream, his rod never had a chance to soften all the way. Once it had returned to its fully bricked state, Raven let him free – but only for a moment. Positioning herself on all fours and poking her juicy ass in the air, Raven looked back at Darrin impatiently.

"Well, what are you waiting for? Come fuck my ass."

"Y-y-you want me to—"

"Did I stutter? I said come fuck me in my fucking ass!" Her voice had raised several notches and Darrin knew she would not take "no" for an answer.

He swallowed hard. He had never imagined himself doing something so sinful and taboo. Although her voice was stern and demanding, she looked back and winked at him playfully, tossing her shiny, long red hair over her shoulder. Raven wiggled her voluptuous backside and Darrin watched her cheeks jiggle in unison. They looked so irresistible. Her pussy and asshole peeked at him, the only parts of her lower half exposed from beneath her sexy lace pantyhose. Darrin laughed and felt himself beginning to loosen up a bit. *God, she is so sexy*, he thought to himself as he got into position behind her. He knew there was no turning back. The fearless sex kitten had him hooked with her naughty, no-holds-barred style and nasty bedroom behavior – and she knew it. She was sure he'd be wrapped around her finger just as she intended. Having sex with Raven felt like Heaven so he just had to experience all she had to offer, even if it meant him going to Hell.

Darrin slowly began inserting his pole into her anal opening. Although it was still wet with the drippings of his previous eruption, his thickness made for an even tighter fit than he imagined. He hesitated, wondering if she might have been in any pain.

"Don't be scared," Raven said. "Give it to me hard. I want it all and I like it rough!"

He carefully inched in deeper, not wanting to disappoint her.

"Did you hear what I said? I said I want it ALL!"

Darrin increased his pace, pushing himself all the way inside until his balls were slapping against her ass.

"Ooooh yeah, like that…but harder," she instructed.

He grabbed her hips and pulled them back toward him as he thrust harder.

"Faster!" Raven yelled. "Give it a good pounding!"

Finally Darrin gripped her cheeks and spread them apart, digging deep and giving her his all.

"Yesssss, that's it. Fuck me goooood, Darrin. Give me all of that big dick!"

Whap! His hand came down onto her backside, startling her. He'd even surprised himself.

"Again," she demanded, strumming her clit like a professional banjo player.

Whap!

"Harder, Darrin."

Whap!

"Harder!"

As he delivered a world-class spanking, Raven furiously rubbed at her pretty pink pearl, bringing her closer to her destination.

"Oooooh, shit!" she screamed as she came, squirting a shower of her juices onto his bed sheets below.

Darrin was right behind her with a toe-curling orgasm of his own. He released his second load all over her plump, round backside, leaving them both satisfied and drained.

Raven sat up in the bed and lit a cigarette, not bothering to ask permission first. She leaned back against the wall, and Darrin watched her take a drag from the cancer stick and slowly exhale the smoke from her lungs. Even with her hair messy from their romp and indulging in a disgusting habit like smoking, he thought she looked absolutely beautiful.

Raven found herself surprisingly pleased by Darrin's performance. *Not bad at all*, she thought to herself. She gave him a mental round of applause, but he'd have to do a lot more than that for her if he wanted a real one.

Chapter Six

Melody hurried into Political Science class five minutes late and scanned the room for Darrin. She spotted him in the most unlikely of places – near the front. She sat down at the open desk beside his and scrupulously eyed him up and down, taking in every inch of his 5'10" physique. She was concerned.

"Hey," she whispered, despite the professor talking in the front of the class. "Where have you been? You haven't called or texted me."

"I've been around." His response was cold...emotionless. He continued to speak, refusing to look in her direction. "Is your phone broken? I don't recall getting any calls or texts from you either."

Melody stared at her boyfriend, shocked by his response and baffled by his unusual nonchalance. She hardly ever called Darrin. As much as he called her, there was no need to. Every day he'd text her "good morning" and would regularly call throughout the day to check up on her. But for the past couple of days, there had been no texts, no calls, no nothing. She continued to stare at the person who seemed more like a stranger than her Darrin.

"You're different, Darrin."

Instead of his normally perfect posture, he was slouching comfortably in his chair with his arm casually hanging over its back. Relaxed fit jeans replaced his stiff, ironed pants. Even his bifocals had been discarded for contact lenses. His entire demeanor was drastically different. Usually uptight and nervous, Darrin was now laid-back and carefree.

"What's gotten into you?" Melody asked, not taking her eyes off of him.

"Nothing, Mel, geez! You're always busy, so I figured you'll call me when you get a chance."

"Well, actually," she smiled, "I'm free this evening if you want to take me—"

"Sorry, no can do," he cut her off. "I'm trying out for the football team today."

Melody couldn't help but laugh. "Seriously, Darrin. The football team?"

But the look he shot back her let her know that he was not joking, and was indeed very serious about it.

* * * * *

Darrin arrived late to tryouts and jogged to the center of the massive field, falling into the line formation with the other determined young Columbia Lions hopefuls.

"You're late," said Coach Turner, glaring at Darrin with a look of irritation.

"I apologize, sir. I—"

"Name?"

"Darrin Brown."

The coach scanned his clipboard once, then twice.

"There's no Darrin Brown on my list."

"I didn't sign up. I kinda decided last minute to try out."

Everyone in attendance snickered, but Coach Turner maintained his hard exterior.

"What position you play, Brown?"

"I don't know yet."

"You...don't...know?" The coach spat each word out one by one, sneering at Darrin as he slowly approached him.

"I've never played before, sir."

More laughter ensued.

"Oh, I see," Coach Turner said nonchalantly, plastering a fake grin on his face. "So you thought you'd just prance out onto my field and try your luck, huh?"

"Well...yeah." Darrin's nonchalance matched the coach's – minus the sarcasm. "That's the idea," he said, being 100 percent honest.

"Get the hell off of my field!" Coach Turner snapped, breaking from his feigned calm and collect state. The sudden outburst startled Darrin.

"Just give me a chance!" Darrin desperately begged. "All my life I've been kept from playing and now that I have the opportunity you're trying to keep me out, too? Don't turn me away, Coach. Not now. All I need is one shot. Please."

Coach Turner saw the desperation in Darrin's eyes. He wouldn't admit it, but for some reason he felt bad for the boy.

"Okay," he shrugged, deciding to show Darrin some sympathy. "If you want to embarrass yourself, that's on you. I could use a good laugh anyway."

* * * * *

After tryouts, Darrin headed back to his dorm feeling on top of the world. He had done great! He performed even better than he expected. Much to the surprise of the coach and everyone else present, Darrin proved to be a skilled and powerful athlete. Despite his average build, he displayed not only exceptional speed and agility, but also incredible strength, tackling skills, and a powerful throwing arm. Coach Turner couldn't believe Darrin had never played football before. Everyone was amazed by his display of sportsmanship, which earned him much respect; even B. Rick, who had taunted him just days earlier, had to shake his hand and congratulate him on a job well done. Darrin had managed to make a few friends and earn the admiration of several female students on the bleachers who had been watching the sweat glisten on his shirtless body as he played. For once in his life, Darrin felt good about himself. He was sure his name would be among those on the list of athletes who made the team.

Women continued ogling him as he strolled bare-chested across the city campus. They whispered to their girlfriends about him, winked flirtatiously, and flashed seductive smiles his way, hoping to get his attention. But none of them were of any interest to him. They weren't Raven. They could never hold a candle to her inextinguishable flame that ran like wildfire, nor the ones she ignited in both his heart and his pants.

Once inside his dorm, Darrin peeled his sweaty jogging pants off and headed for the shower. With the testosterone still raging through him, he badly wished Raven was there to relieve him.

After turning off the shower, Darrin exited the steam-filled bathroom with a towel wrapped around his waist. He selected a pair of blue plaid boxer shorts and dropped his towel. Before stepping into his underwear, he stopped to admire his naked body in the mirror. He curled his arm tightly and watched his bicep muscle rise.

"Nice," a sultry voice called out from his bed. It was Raven. She was laid atop his comforter spread eagle, the delicate fingers of her right hand gently stroking her treasure box while the other raised a lit cigarette to her parted lips.

She looked at him with a come-hither stare that made words unnecessary. He walked to her, stroking his hardening member. Her nipples were firm; milk chocolate twins that seemed to be staring at him, begging to be tasted. His tongue greeted one; French-kissing it as it if could kiss him back.

Then, the other – he provided it with the same attention so as not to make the first one jealous. He smiled at the thought.

"Lie down," said Raven as she blew the last of the cigarette smoke from her lungs and rudely butted the stump out on his bedside table.

He eagerly obliged, one hand lustfully stroking his shaft while he placed the other behind his head and closed his eyes, readily anticipating her touch. He wasn't expecting her to sit on his face, but that is exactly what she did.

Her faucet was already leaking, trickling down into his mouth and onto his face. Like a striking cobra, his tongue sprang from his mouth. It slithered its way into her flower, thirsty for more of its nectar. The intense sweetness made his taste buds tingle. His tongue fervently wriggled about, desperate to fulfill its insatiable craving for more, and Darrin soon began sucking like a starving infant at its mother's breast. Abandoning all civility, he slurped every drop that spilled from her opening, drinking from her well as if quenching his dying thirst. Raven felt his tongue spiraling around the inside of her walls. She fucked his tongue savagely, determined to give him more of the cream filling he so desired. Squeezing her eyes shut, she announced that she was coming and blissfully spewed out a mouthful of Darrin's new favorite beverage.

Chapter Seven

Raven spotted Darrin walking out of class with Melody. She watched from a distance as Melody kissed him on his cheek and the two parted ways. Darrin's face lit up when Raven approached him.

"Your girlfriend?" she asked nonchalantly, already knowing the answer.

"Yeah, the ol' ball and chain." Darrin rolled his eyes.

"She's cute. But anyway, congratulations are in order. I hear you're one of the newest Columbia Lions."

"Really?!" His eyes illuminated with the excitement of a 5-year-old boy on Christmas morning. "The list is out?"

"Yep. There's one posted up right over here."

Darrin eagerly followed Raven down the hall, staying closely on her heels like a loyal puppy. She pointed to his name at the top of the list of students who successfully made the Lions roster.

"Yesss!" he proudly exclaimed, jumping up and punching the air above him before turning his attention back to her. "Oh Raven, I don't know what to say. I've always wanted this and I owe it all to you. Thank you! There's no way I could've done it without you. How can I repay you?"

"Calm down, Darrin. You'll have your chance soon enough."

Darrin knew that Raven was the reason for him feeling like a new man. Before meeting her he was a weak, introverted loner; a scared little boy who would have never had the guts to try out for the football team. But ever since that first night with Raven, something inside him had changed. He no longer sulked around campus invisibly. He now walked with a masculine strut, spoke in a firm tone of voice, and went throughout his day with confidence and purpose. His days of sitting around waiting for Melody to make time for him were over. Where she was merely a girl to him, Raven was a woman; the woman of his dreams and the woman he loved. In his heart he genuinely felt that he and Raven were soul mates. He felt indebted to her and bound to her for eternity.

"How can I ever repay you, Raven?" he repeated the question. "I'll do anything for you…anything in the world."

"Anything?" asked Raven, her lips curling into a wicked smile.

* * * * *

It didn't take long for Melody to notice that something had drastically changed with Darrin. Determined to get to the bottom of it, she decided to stop by his dorm one night to sit down for a heart-to-heart.

"Okay, so cut the crap, Darrin. What's up with you lately? You're different."

"It's nothing, Melody. I'm just growing up. I was tired of being the loser that I was. I would think you'd be happy for me."

"I am! I mean, don't get me wrong, I think the newfound confidence you have now is great. And I'm glad you've come out of your shell and grown more comfortable with who you are. But you're distant now. I hardly ever hear from you anymore, and when I see you it's like…it's like your mind is somewhere else." Melody glanced up at Darrin to see him dreamily gazing out the window, illustrating the very point she had just made. "Darrin, are you listening to me?!"

"I hear you, Mel, okay?"

"Is there someone else?"

"Huh?"

"Is there another woman? Is that why you're acting this way?"

"No," he lied. "Well, yes…but it's not like that."

Melody sassily threw her hands on her hips as her eyes widened. "Who is she?"

"She's a friend from one of my classes – but that's it! Just a friend, I swear."

Melody knew Darrin was not the type to lie. She seriously doubted that he would cheat on her. After all, he was a man of God. Still, she couldn't help being somewhat suspicious of his mystery female "friend" and how she'd managed to cause the radical changes apparent in Darrin.

"Well, when do I get to meet her? You don't have a problem with us meeting, do you? I'm sure you must have told her about me."

"Yeah sure, she knows all about you. And I think it will be a great idea if you two meet. You'll love her."

Chapter Eight

"Now I need you be open-minded, Mel," said Darrin, as they stepped off the L train at Bedford Avenue station in the Williamsburg section of Brooklyn. "Like I said, Raven's a little different, but don't judge her by her appearance. I promise this will be a new and exciting experience."

He grabbed her hand and led her through the windy October night until they reached their destination several blocks away.

Melody giggled as they ascended the steps of what appeared to be an old, vacant Catholic cathedral. She was giddy with excitement. "What is this, Darrin? Some type of Halloween attraction? A haunted house thing?"

"Something like that," he smiled. He knocked on the weathered door and fragments of its chipping red paint fell to the ground below as it rattled in its decaying frame. Moments later, Raven opened the door.

"Welcome," she greeted the two of them. "Come inside."

As soon as she set eyes on Raven, Melody found herself envious of her incomparable beauty. She felt extremely insecure in her presence as she and Darrin entered the huge dilapidated building and took in their surroundings. Most of the rows of pews in the church had been removed and the scarce lighting provided by candles just barely illuminated the few remaining pieces of furniture scattered around the grime-covered sanctuary.

"You must be Melody. Nice to finally meet you."

"Likewise," Melody said, forcing a smile as she looked over Raven's hourglass figure outfitted in black modern gothic attire. Although she'd never say it out loud, she had to admit to herself, the woman's body was pure perfection.

"Follow me, guys."

Melody watched Raven's swaying hips as she led them across the room, down what they imagined used to serve as the aisle for church-goers many years ago.

"I'm nervous, Darrin," Melody whispered to him, clutching his arm tightly. "This place is creepy."

"Don't worry," Raven said, spinning around. "There's nothing to be afraid of. I promise it'll be fun." She stopped to remove a steel flask from the inside pocket of her coat and offered it to Melody. "Here, take a sip. It'll make you feel better."

"Oh, no thank you," Melody declined. "I don't drink."

"All you need is a little sip to ease your fears. Look…" Raven took a long swig from the flask before passing it to Darrin who followed suit.

"You drink now, Darrin?" asked Melody, surprised.

"Come on, Mel. You said you'd keep an open mind. We're grown now. And it's just one little sip. It's impossible to get drunk off of one sip. I don't even feel that l'il drop I just had."

"Plus," Raven added, "It's not as if it's some kind of sin or something. Even Jesus drank. Hell, he liked to drink so much he turned water to wine!"

The three of them shared a laugh and Melody took the flask from Darrin and downed a big gulp. "Yuck!" She stuck out her tongue, turned up her face, and passed the disgusting-tasting elixir back to Raven who tucked it safely away.

Within a matter of minutes Melody began to feel the affects of the drink. The room started to spin and she felt lightheaded.

"I think I'm gonna pass out. I need to lie down."

"Of course. Right over here," said Raven, pointing to the pulpit several feet ahead of them.

Raven and Darrin attempted to help Melody walk, but her steps were slow and shaky, causing her to stumble and fall.

"Get her up," Raven impatiently demanded. Without hesitation Darrin did as he was told, hoisting Melody up and throwing her over his shoulder. They made their way down the remainder of the aisle and ascended the short set of stairs leading to the wooden pulpit. Illuminated by dozens of candles, it was the most well-lit area of the church; and though her vision was clouded and the room was spinning, Melody was able to take in sporadic imagery of the upside down crosses and various animal skulls that adorned the filthy walls. Paintings and sculptures of what appeared to be acts of sex, murder, and sacrifice were also part of the bizarre décor, along with indecipherable Latin and Aramaic phrases written on the walls. The rickety floorboards creaked as they walked, drawing Melody's attention downward. There she noticed markings drawn in white chalk on the weathered, dark hardwood floor beneath them.

"You can lay her down right here," Raven announced. Upon examining the markings closer, Melody could tell they were standing directly in the center of a huge eye within a pentagram. That is all she was able to make out before Darrin laid her down on top of it.

Without warning, Raven began undressing. She stripped down to nude before climbing on top of Melody and unbuttoning her pants as well. Melody tried her hardest to get up and to protest; she wanted more than anything to push Raven off of her and scream for her to get the hell away from her, but she was unable to move or speak. Though her muscles were paralyzed, eyesight was blurry, and thoughts were hazy, she remained conscious. Part of her wondered if it was a dream. But another part was sure the sick act occurring was very real. Helpless and afraid, a lone tear slid down the side of her face. Raven palmed Melody's small, perky breasts, squeezing them firmly and thumbing her nipples before taking one into her mouth. She sucked the bud of flesh it until it stood erect before diverting her attention to the other. While tending to Melody's nipples with her tongue, Raven reached her hand downward and inserted a finger into her slit. Displeased with the lack of moisture, her head moved southbound. She positioned her face between Melody's legs, allowing her tongue to part the smooth lower lips. Holding her legs back, Raven sucked and licked Melody's clitoris until at last the cream flowed onto her tongue. She was interrupted by the sensation of Darrin's hands on her hips from behind her. She turned just as he was inching forward to insert his rock hard dick.

"Uh-uh-uh," said Raven, crawling upwards. "That's for Melody. Be a good boy now and fill her up nice for me." Darrin's disappointment was apparent on his face as he frowned sadly.

"But Raven, can I least taste you?"

"I suppose," she sighed, rolling her eyes. Still straddling Melody, Raven arched her back, leaving her ass in the air as she dove downward to return her wet mouth to Melody's hardened nipples. Darrin reluctantly forced himself inside of Melody, but immediately found the sensation of her slick, tight virgin hole extremely pleasurable. As he stroked her narrow passage, he devoured Raven savagely from behind, sliding his tongue all over and inside her love box. He was turned on even more by the moans of ecstasy she emitted and the sexiness of her voice as she coached him.

"Fuck that pussy, Darrin! Give her all of that big, hard dick!"

"Yes, Raven."

"I want you to cum all in that pussy," she said matter-of-factly. "Make sure you're in balls deep."

"Yes, Raven."

Melody had eventually drifted off into a state of unconsciousness, but that didn't deter Raven or Darrin one bit.

"Fuck her harder! Enjoy that virgin twat. I know it's nice and wet. She was dripping in my mouth. I licked the little bitch good."

"Am I licking you good, Raven?"

"Mmmm, yes you are. Good boy. Now move your tongue up and lick my asshole."

Darrin immediately obeyed.

"Put your tongue in it. Yesss, just like that."

Though the sensation of taking Melody's virginity felt amazing, nothing brought Darrin more pleasure than pleasing Raven. Her seductive voice coupled with the delicious flavor of her body and the sight of her thick, juicy ass, had him nearing the edge of his peak. Raven could sense he was near climax as his strokes quickened and intensified.

"Now give her that nut, Darrin! Fill that tight little pussy right up and don't you dare waste one drop!"

Darrin screamed out Raven's name as he erupted like a geyser, releasing his hot load deep inside of Melody, just as he had been instructed.

Making sure to follow all of Raven's twisted directions, he didn't pull out until he was certain every single drop had been excreted and his rod fell limp.

* * * * *

The following morning a naked Melody sprung up in Darrin's bed sweating profusely and breathing heavily, startling him out of his sleep.

"What's wrong, Mel? You okay?"

"Last night!" she yelled, jumping out of bed and backing away from him fearfully.

"Don't tell me you're regretting it now. I know we said we'd wait for marriage but—"

"How could you, Darrin?! You and that sick bitch, Raven!"

"Calm down, Melody. What are you talking about?"

"Oh, you're just gonna pretend it didn't happen? I can feel it. I'm so sore down there!"

"Of course you might be a little sore. It was your first time. But Raven had nothing to do with it. We had a little bit to drink and you said you didn't feel good so we left the church and came back to spend the night here. You and I had a beautiful first time. You really don't remember it?"

Melody could see the obvious pain in Darrin's eyes as they looked back into hers. He was crushed. How could she admit that she had been so drunk she had absolutely no recollection of their first time together? She realized the whole memory of the night before at the abandoned cathedral was nothing more than a bad, alcohol-induced nightmare. She calmed herself down and joined Darrin back in bed, laughing and shaking her head at her own irrationality and silliness.

"Don't mind me, babe. I had the strangest, craziest, most outrageous dream last night! It felt so real. I guess that's what liquor can do to your mind. Sorry for tripping. But promise me you'll never, *ever* let me drink again!"

"I promise," Darrin chuckled, comforting her in his arms.

Chapter Nine

Two months later, Darrin clutched Melody's sweaty hand as she sat nervously on a gynecologist's examination table waiting for the doctor to enter the room. Within moments, the 50-ish balding man entered wearing a tight-lipped smile.

"Well, looks like you two are going to have a baby," he said, confirming Melody's worst fear. "Congratulations!"

"Oh, nooooo!" Melody wailed, burying her face into Darrin's shoulder.

She had suspected there was a possibility she could be with child after missing her last period and experiencing tenderness in her breasts.

"How far along is she, Doctor?" asked Darrin, beaming a proud father-to-be grin.

"Melody is about eight weeks pregnant, giving her an estimated due date of July 6th."

Once Melody had finished crying, talking to the doctor, and scheduling her next prenatal appointment, she and Darrin headed back to campus.

"Darrin, we're going to have to get married as soon as possible."

"Whoa! Slow down, Mel. We haven't even told our parents yet. Why don't you call your mom and dad and let them know they have a grandbaby on the way?"

Dreading having to break the news to her parents, Melody decided to put the call off until later, and Darrin was happy to have escaped the marriage conversation, if only for a while. He knew there was no way he could possibly marry Melody. The baby wouldn't change a thing. In his eyes, Raven was still the only woman for him.

* * * * *

As the months passed, Darrin and Melody continued their lives as usual. They maintained their good grades and Melody refused to let her pregnancy keep her from her student organizations and activities.

To Darrin's dismay, however, Raven had disappeared completely. Every Monday, Wednesday, and Friday he looked for her in class, hopeful that she'd come strutting through the door. But each time he was let down, faced with disappointment when she failed to show. After the night in the old church, he had neither seen nor heard from her again.

When classes ended in May, Darrin and Melody decided to spend the summer in New York in lieu of returning to Detroit. Melody claimed she wanted to stay because she was happy with her New

York obstetrician and wanted him to deliver the baby. But truth be told, she stayed to spite her parents, who'd been unrelenting in voicing their disapproval of her decision to have pre-marital relations ever since they learned of the pregnancy. Darrin had his own reason for wanting to stay; he wanted to stick around NYC in hopes that Raven would one day return. So the two of them used their financial aid refunds to rent a small one-bedroom apartment in Brooklyn, and Darrin took on a job at a local coffee shop in order to support them.

* * * * *

Before they knew it July had rolled around. It was a sweltering summer, and the backaches, swollen feet, and waddling around with 40 extra pounds of weight in 98-degree weather made for one miserable Melody. She was eagerly awaiting the arrival of the baby – a girl that she planned on naming Shannon.

Darrin, on the other hand, was not feeling quite as optimistic about their daughter's impending birth. The initial excitement of fatherhood had long worn off and the thought of being a dad now had him extremely nervous. Already overwhelmed with bills and work, he knew things would only get worse once the baby arrived, and even more so when the fall semester started several weeks after. Above all Darrin was depressed that Raven had not returned. He hadn't intended to get Melody pregnant that night. He was only following Raven's instructions to please her.

"Now look at this mess I've gotten myself into," he grumbled to himself while finishing up mopping the floors at work one rainy night. "All this bullshit I have to deal with and Raven is nowhere to be found."

The door chime sounded, letting him know that someone had entered the shop.

"We're closed," he said grumpily, setting down the mop and picking up the bucket of grimy water. The customer's shoes click-clacked across the shiny linoleum floor as they ignored his statement and walked toward him.

"Did you hear me?" Darrin asked, annoyed, turning to look at the unwanted guest that was tracking dirty water all over the freshly mopped floor. "I said we're closed."

The visitor was wearing a long, black hooded cloak; drops of rainwater dripped from its soaking fabric onto the floor.

"Closed even for me?" the patron asked, removing the hood.

"Raven!" yelled Darrin ecstatically, dropping the bucket and running over to embrace her. "Where have you been?"

Raven held her hand up, halting his gait and gesturing for him to calm down. She removed her cloak and hung it over the back of a chair before sitting in another and crossing her shapely, latex-clad legs. Darrin followed suit, taking in her exceptional beauty and skintight ensemble.

"You're still as gorgeous as ever."

"How's Melody?" she asked, ignoring Darrin's compliment.

"Fine," he unenthusiastically replied.

"And the baby?"

"She's fine too," he said, rolling his eyes.

"Oh, it's a girl? How nice. So she's due just about any day now, right?"

"Unfortunately."

"You're not excited about the baby?"

"Not exactly. I didn't mean to get Melody pregnant, Raven. I was just doing what you told me to do. I only wanted to please you. And then you disappeared on me. Where have you been all this time? Why'd you just up and leave without a word?"

"Don't you ever dare question me!" she snapped. "Do you understand?"

"Yes, Raven," he responded sheepishly. "I'm so sorry. I just really missed you."

"Where I've been is none of your concern. I'm back now. And if you don't do what I say you'll never see me again. Now listen closely..."

Darrin moved to the edge of his seat listening intently to Raven's every word.

VANNA B.

Chapter Ten

Once he reached home, Darrin took a quick hot shower to wash away the day. It had been a long one and he was exhausted. Melody was already sound asleep and he was glad. He'd be able to go to sleep without having to hear her nagging and complaining. He slowly slipped into the soft, comfy bed next to Melody, trying his hardest not to wake her. Once his head hit the pillow, he relaxed his tense muscles and settled down with a deep exhale. It only took a few short minutes for him to drift off and join her in slumber.

As soon as his brain fell into REM sleep, a vivid dream began to play out in his mind. The star of the dream, of course, was Raven. In his dream, just as she had done earlier that evening, she walked into the coffee shop in her long, black hooded cloak, tracking water across the floor. When she reached Darrin the cloak dropped to the floor, revealing her wet, naked body. Her skin glistened as drops of rainwater ran down her curves. She reached into Darrin's uniform pants and freed his hardened cock. Instantly, she dropped to her knees, taking the tip of his penis into her mouth. She sucked ferociously as if she might devour him whole at any moment. Raven stroked his shaft up and down with her tongue, licking it like a melting ice cream cone on a sizzling August afternoon. He grabbed the back of her head and thrust deep into her throat. Hands free, she took in the entire length of his manhood as thick saliva dripped from her mouth. Darrin could feel her tongue tickling the bottom of his scrotum. On the verge of climax, he removed himself from her throat. As if reading his mind, Raven spun around and bent over a table, placing one knee on the tabletop and balancing herself on the other leg. Darrin entered her wetness with one forceful thrust of his hips and showed no mercy as he pounded her tightness with all the vigor he could muster. She screamed out her pleasure as she arched her back and pushed her hips back toward him, enjoying each and every powerful stoke.

"Oooooh baby, I love you!" Raven yelled out as she orgasmed. Darrin could feel his semen nearing the surface. "Yes, fuck me, Darrin! Yessss! AHHHHHH!"

"AHHHHHH!" He awakened to Melody's high-pitched screams. She always found a way to annoy him; this time having interrupted the impending climax to his wonderful wet dream.

"Shit," he mumbled to himself, throwing the covers back and stumbling out of bed. He followed Melody's terrified voice into the bathroom, where she was down on the floor, holding her belly as she leaned back against the bathtub in tears.

"Darrin, the baby is coming!" she cried. "I can't get up. It hurts so bad!"

Darrin helped her up off of the floor and back onto the bed.

"I'm gonna call for an ambulance. Just breathe and try to calm down."

"I caaan't," she wailed pitifully. "This pain is killing me! I don't think I'm gonna make it."

"Here," Darrin said, handing her a pill he retrieved from the nightstand drawer. "Take this. It'll help with the pain." With no hesitation or questioning Melody snatched the small pill from Darrin's hand and popped it into her mouth. Desperate for relief from the excruciating pain, she dry swallowed the pill, while Darrin called for the ambulance.

VANNA B.

Chapter Eleven

Melody opened her eyes and blinked several times to clear her blurry vision. The room was dark and silent. Lying on her back she felt a cold, hard surface beneath her naked body. She looked up into the blackness, trying to recall where she was and how she got there. The last thing she could remember is being back at the apartment suffering from terribly painful contractions. *The baby!* She frantically grabbed at her stomach with both hands and gasped in shock at what felt like stitches across her lower abdomen. The entire area was tender; she winced in pain as her fingertips rolled across her aching, barren belly. In a panic, she quickly sat up, cringing at the intense pain that shot from her womb to the rest of her body. Through the darkness, she squinted at her stomach until finally her eyes adjusted and she was able to see. Sure enough, there was a line of small X's threaded through her skin; sloppy stitches apparently done by amateur hands sealed an incision where her baby girl was removed. Between her shivering legs, Melody noticed something on the floor: the familiar chalk markings of an eye within a pentagram. A chill shook her naked body. Every hair on her weakened frame stood on end. Melody screamed out in horror, realizing she was once again inside of the creepy abandoned cathedral. It hadn't been a dream at all. The horrible incident she had foolishly brushed off as a drunken nightmare nine months ago had actually occurred.

"Raven!" she yelled out, crying uncontrollably, her fear-stricken voice echoing in the large, empty shell of a building. "What have you done, you sick bitch!? Where's my BABY?!"

Despite the excruciating pain, she coaxed her tingly limbs to life and forced herself to stand. Moving forward, she stumbled from the center of the chalk drawings.

"I knew you drugged me that night! If you've hurt my baby in any way I swear to God I'll kill you!"

Melody staggered past a large, ornate gold chair with black velvet cushioning and over to the old podium standing on the pulpit. On it sat a silver dagger, white towels, and rusty surgical tools – all stained with fresh blood. Beneath them lied several thick, dusty books. Melody lifted up the topmost one, examining the page to which it was opened. One passage, underlined in red, immediately stuck out to her. She began to read.

Worshipping the Goddess Lilith - The Sacrificial Moon Ritual:
Under the Waning Crescent Moon each coven must offer as a sacrifice to the Goddess Mother the beating heart of a newborn conceived and birthed by a virgin mother on the unholy grounds.

The air left her lungs. Feeling faint, Melody fell to the floor. She clutched her bare chest and gasped for air, struggling to breathe.

"No, no, no!" she repeated over and over shaking her head in denial. "It can't be," she whispered, her hand cupping over her mouth as her eyes widened in panic. With her back against the wooden podium and her face in her hands, Melody sat, crying hysterically.

She was overcome with sorrow – and rage. With anger bubbling over, she peered up at the ceiling above and screamed, "How could you let this happen?!" She sought answers, but there was no response. There was nothing up there but impenetrable blackness. The only thing to be heard was the echoing of her lonely, hopeless cries.

Melody felt she had been cheated and duped by her religion…let down by faith…abandoned by the God she loyally worshipped. Despite it all, He had let the unthinkable happen. Her baby girl was gone. Demonic forces were heavy at play – a greater evil than she ever imagined existed. They had won. Evil had unfairly prevailed over good. She felt maleficence and immorality all around her. They seemed to be closing in on her. She had to get out of there.

Mustering her strength once more, Melody stood to her feet with unrelenting determination and purpose. She yanked the black tablecloth from the long table beside the podium, causing dozens of unlabeled bottles containing colorful mystery liquids to shatter to the floor. She wrapped the tablecloth around her lacerated body before grabbing the book and bolting out of the church.

ChaPteR Twelve

"I need help!" Melody yelled running into the police precinct several blocks from the church.

"What's the matter, Miss?" Officer Foley asked standing from his seat at the front desk. He suspiciously eyed her disheveled appearance and unconventional choice of attire as he cautiously stepped around the desk and approached her.

"She stole my baby!" Melody cried frantically.

"Okay now, take it easy. Calm down and tell me what happened. Who took your baby?"

"Her name is Raven! An evil succubus and baby-murdering witch named Raven! She seduced my boyfriend into drugging me and then she cut my baby girl from my womb to sacrifice her! You've got to help me. My baby may still be alive. We have to find her! Please!"

Foley shifted his eyes to Officer Leeks who only briefly pried his eyes from his New York Post to look Melody up and down before diverting his attention back to the newspaper.

"Raving lunatic," Leeks coughed into his palm sarcastically, drawing a few chuckles from several other cops in the station.

Melody's hands grabbed the sides of her throbbing head to stop the room from spinning.

Losing her balance, she gripped the front desk for stability.

"Miss, are you under the influence of any drugs or alcohol?" Foley asked.

"What? No! I'm not drunk or high, and I'm not crazy! I'm telling you the truth. Look…" She set the book on the front counter, pointing to the underlined passage for him to read. "There's an old abandoned cathedral a couple blocks up on Kent Ave. If you look there you'll find the knife she used to cut me open and the tools she used to stitch—"

Mid-sentence, Melody's eyes rolled to the ceiling as she fell unconscious, hitting the floor like a ton of bricks. The tablecloth wrapped around her slipped down in the process.

"Get a medic squad over here!" Foley yelled. Officer Leeks dropped his newspaper to assist Foley with raising Melody's limp body from the floor. They exchanged looks of horror once they saw her exposed stomach bleeding through the nasty looking makeshift stitches.

Chapter Thirteen

Officers Foley and Leeks were unsure what to make of Melody's outrageous claims. The only thing they were sure of is that all that business about witches and sacrifices had to be a bunch of malarkey. But after seeing that she'd obviously been cut open and stitched up by someone other than a doctor, they decided they should at least check the church out.

On the brief ride over, Foley flipped through the large book Melody had been carrying.

"This is some crazy shit," he said to Leeks. "Listen to this." He began to read from a passage:

Any succubus of the coven may maintain a youthful appearance, regardless of age, by milking the semen of a virgin male. Said male will then be at her disposal, bound for eternity by feelings of love and lust.

"No shit," said Leeks as he pulled the squad car up to the church and placed it in park. "I think my mistress may be a damn succubus then." The two officers laughed as they exited the vehicle.

Foley and Leeks entered the dilapidated old church nonchalantly, flashlights in hand. They ascended the long aisle up to the front of the sanctuary, inspecting the large, seemingly empty abandoned building. Upon approaching the pulpit, they noticed a lone figure sitting in a throne-like chair beneath a cloud of smoke.

"NYPD! Hands where we can see 'em!" Leeks ordered as they both quickly removed their weapons from their holsters, taking aim.

Raven rose from her seated position and seductively strutted toward them, prompting them to ease their weapons down at the breathtaking sight of her beautiful nude body.

"Mmmmm," she purred sadistically. "How I love a man in uniform."

VANNA B.

ChaPteR One

It had been exactly three months since Darrin had seen Raven. It seemed like an eternity though, as he counted each lonely day that passed. He started every morning enthusiastically, hoping it would be the day she returned to him, but was always met with the same sad, disappointing end.

Raven had explicitly instructed Darrin not to seek her out. He was to wait until she came for him. In the meantime, he was to keep his love muscle strong for her by engaging it whenever the mood struck him. He couldn't believe Raven was telling him to sleep with other women, but he obeyed her twisted request as he did all of her orders – without question. Every night he had a different woman in his bed to quench the insatiable desire brought on by his constant longing for Raven. Of course, none of his one-night stands could ever measure up to her in his eyes, but it was better than blue balls or resorting to his "right hand man," he reasoned.

At the three-month mark, Darrin began to wonder if Raven would ever return. His heart beat quadruple time, his breaths quickened, and his palms dampened with perspiration; the mere thought of never seeing her again sent him into a panic. He decided enough was enough. He *had* to go to her. He hoped Raven wouldn't be too upset by his disobedience. She knew how he felt about her – perhaps she'd understand.

Darrin apprehensively ran his boar bristle brush through his jet-black waves as he walked up the crumbling cement steps of what was left of the old abandoned cathedral. The crisp October air had the tip of his nose and ears numb. The temperature felt exactly as it did the year prior when he ascended the same steps with Melody. He remembered it vividly. He realized he was as nervous as she had been then, but quickly laughed the thought away. Darrin paused just outside the entrance to straighten out his clothes and adjust his posture one final time before pushing the rickety door open. Inside the church was dark and empty. He entered the blackness and his careful steps echoed in the large hollow building.

"Hello?" he called out. "Raven, are you in here?"

There was no response; just the echoes of his own voice bouncing off of the four walls and 20-foot ceiling. Defeated, Darrin turned to leave. But the sound of a piano playing stopped him in his tracks. He looked in the direction of the music where he noticed the faintest flickers of light dancing beneath a closed door he failed to spot during his last visit. He slowly opened the door and followed the piano music down a long, tunnel-like hallway. He wasn't prepared for what he saw at the end of it.

There, bent over an antique baby grand piano, was Raven, getting pounded from behind by a 6'3" Fabio wannabe. The sound of random keys being mashed prevented them from hearing him enter, and they continued fucking like wild animals right before his eyes. Darrin was stunned; his muscles froze up and everything seemed to move in slow motion. He was unable to do anything but stand there in the doorway watching in horror as the long-haired, Herculean pretty boy drove his 11 inches of meat deep into the love of his life. Her knees never left their firmly planted position on the piano bench and he never took his hands off her perfectly round ass. Raven's breasts bounced up and down as he rammed her harder and harder. Sweat rolled down his flexing muscular body, and his stiff, veined cock glistened in the candlelight with Raven's cream. Darrin opened his mouth to speak but no words came out. He felt his heart was breaking. He squeezed his eyes shut, unable to bear the sight before him. But he could still hear Raven's squeals of pleasure.

"Yes, Claude! Fuck me good! Mmmmmm, yeah baby!"

Despite her screaming out another man's name, Darrin felt weak at the sound of her voice. Her sweet, sultry tone was always music to his ears. Then Claude's loudening moans invaded his eardrums. It was like nails across a chalkboard. Darrin opened his eyes and was promptly snapped back to reality. Claude thrust one final time and spewed a huge load inside of Raven before removing himself from her dripping, throbbing cunt. That's when Darrin lost it.

Darrin yelled out in rage as he charged Claude, tackling the unsuspecting man to the floor before his dick even had a chance to go limp. Claude held up his large, chiseled arms to block Darrin's incoming punches before throwing back several of his own.

"Okay, that's enough you two," Raven said calmly, lighting a cigarette.

But the two men continued to go at it.

"I said," Raven raised her voice accordingly, "knock it the fuck off!"

The men froze obediently, each refusing to look away as they stood their ground with flaring nostrils and heaving chests.

"What the fuck are you doing here, Darrin?" Raven asked, her annoyance obvious in her voice. She picked up the bottle of Jack Daniels next to the bench and swallowed a mouthful of the fiery liquid before continuing. "Don't you have better things to do, like tend to Melody?"

"Melody? I haven't seen her since the sacrifice. I don't know her whereabouts and I don't care."

"Okay, so again…what the fuck are you doing here? I gave you very simple instructions; instructions that did not involve *you* coming *here*." She put emphasis on "you" and "here," pointing her finger at him and the floor as she sternly delivered the words.

"Raven, I'm sorry," he said with apologetic eyes as he dropped to his knees. "I know you said to wait until you came for me but I just couldn't bear it any longer. I missed you too much. I love you!"

"I love you more!" Claude piped up.

"You shut the hell up!" Darrin fired at him.

"Both of you quiet down now!" yelled Raven. "You're giving me a fucking headache." She took a long drag of her cigarette and watched as the two men continued their stand off, staring one another down with rage-filled glares.

"Hmmm," Raven hummed, allowing her glossed lips to stretch into her signature sinister grin. "I have an idea. You both say you love me the most?" She bit her thumbnail in excitement. "I want you to prove it by fighting for me – to the death. I have a very important task I need completed and whoever wins will be the one that gets to do it for me."

VANNA B.

Chapter Two

Raven sat on the bench and leaned her naked body back, resting her elbows on the piano. Once she was in a relaxed position, she crossed her smooth brown legs, preparing for the show. She tossed back the bottle of whiskey and chugged down a fifth of its contents before impatiently asking, "What are you two idiots waiting for? Fight, motherfuckers."

Eager to obey, Darrin once again attacked Claude with no regard for his nudity. This time, however, Claude had the chance to see him coming. He sprung into a fighting stance and wasted no time introducing his bear-like fists to Darrin's facial features. Claude was incredibly strong. Darrin possessed strength as well, but Claude's size and muscle mass allowed him to put some serious power into his punches. Darrin soon became dazed by the repeated blows to the head, but he shook it off as best he could and focused on maintaining his footing. He countered Claude's hooks and jabs with punches of his own, although the few of them that landed did little damage. Darrin was far from a fighter. He had never even been in a physical altercation before. But he was determined. He was fighting for Raven; as far as he was concerned, defeat was not an option. He knew all he had to do was put mind over matter. Despite the beating he was taking, he refused to give in. Claude continued to send a brutal barrage of blows raining down on Darrin, and Darrin gradually felt his energy draining and his body weakening. The adrenaline racing through his veins prevented him from noticing the pain much, but he was winded – and so was Claude. He took several steps back to catch his breath and Darrin did the same. The men's eyes moved from one another to Raven and the sight of her immediately energized them.

"I'm through toying with you, boy," Claude growled, eager to finish Darrin off and become the victor. He rushed at Darrin with all the force within him. Darrin snatched the Jack Daniels bottle from Raven's hand and smashed it over Claude's head, drenching his long hair and upper body in the strong-smelling liquor. Claude was momentarily stunned and Darrin did not hesitate to take advantage of the opportunity. This was his chance to make his move. He drove what was left of the broken bottle right into Claude's thick neck, and the jagged glass sliced a three-inch gash into his throat. Claude dropped to his knees, desperately clenching his neck with both hands. Blood began filling his lungs. It oozed from between his fingers, splattering onto the floor beneath him. He fell over, his head hitting the hardwood floor with a loud thud. His eyes locked on Raven as he struggled to breathe. When the continually expanding pool of blood beneath him reached the tips of Raven's toes she looked down at it, enjoying its warmth and admiring how it matched the deep shade of red painted onto her toenails. She and Darrin's glares were colder than the arctic as they stared into the dying man's eyes, watching his life slip away with emotionless stillness. There wasn't a trace of pity on their stony faces – not even when he took his last breath.

"Nice, Darrin," Raven praised him as she walked through the blood and stepped over Claude's lifeless body. "You owe me a bottle of whiskey."

VANNA B.

Chapter Three

"Darrin, the anniversary of my summoning is approaching," Raven said as she slipped on her floor-length, black silk robe.

Darrin stared at her with a puzzled look that said he had no clue what she was speaking of.

"It's sort of like my birthday, only I wasn't actually born. I was summoned from Hell."

"Summoned? But by who? And why?"

Raven huffed and rolled her eyes as if she was annoyed by his questions. But in actuality, there were very few things that pleased her more than talking about herself.

"I was called upon by a group of voodoo priestesses in Haiti back in 1791," she explained. "They were slaves desperate for freedom. There was a man the high priestess prophesied was the one that would get the slaves to organize and rise up against the French."

"You're taking about Toussaint Louverture."

"Once again your academically-attained knowledge betrays you. Toussaint may have led the rebellion, but there may never even have been one if it wasn't for Dutty Boukman. He's the one who exhorted the oppressed Haitians into uprising. He instilled the spirit of fight and defiance that moved

Toussaint and the others into starting the Haitian Revolution…thanks to me."

Darrin listened intently as Raven spoke, eager to know her role in the great historic event.

"Dutty was strong and extremely intelligent. Also a voodoo priest himself, he was a powerful man. Even though the high priestess knew he was the one, Dutty had doubts. I was called upon to erase those doubts."

Darrin sat enthralled by Raven's story as she continued.

"By the time I was done with him he knew what to do and how to do it. There were thousands of slave owners dead by the end of the week. And when they killed Dutty, shit really hit the fan. They hung his head in the middle of Saint-Domingue hoping it would put an end to the movement. But it was too late. By then the slaves felt they were unstoppable and proved that sentiment to be true. Dutty's death increased their rage tenfold and only added fuel to the fire of their unbreakable spirit."

"Wow," Darrin whispered, his eyes the size of silver dollars. "That's amazing."

"Yes, quite. So anyway, as I was saying, in a week I'll have been on Earth for 221 years and it'll be time for my yearly feast."

"What'll you be having?" he asked, expecting her to name some fancy restaurant or her favorite gourmet dinner.

"Hearts," she replied. "I need thirteen hearts every year to ensure my eternal life. And you're going to fetch them for me."

"Of course, Raven. Whatever you want."

"I want them fresh; you're to bring them to me immediately and be sure to keep them warm during transport."

"I will."

"I have a week to consume all thirteen of them so I *must* have them all before next Friday. Do you understand? And most importantly, female hearts only! Men are too fucking stupid. I won't take any chances eating that garbage."

"Yes, Raven."

"Now go and get started right away."

VANNA B.

Chapter Four

Darrin wasted no time embarking on his mission. *This will be a piece of cake*, he thought to himself as he exited the church. Over the last few months he had become accustomed to picking up random women and bedding them the same night. The newfound confidence Raven had helped him discover made him a magnet for women of all sorts. That, coupled with his good looks, laid back swagger, and charming smile, caused members of the opposite sex to gravitate to him.

Darrin decided on one of the bars he frequented several blocks from his apartment. It was late on a Friday night, so the place was sure to be busy. He strolled in and took a seat at the bar before nodding his greeting to his favorite bartender, Sam. He noticed a group of young ladies partying at the other end of the bar. The way they were letting loose and dancing with one another let him know they were about three or four rounds in.

"How's it goin' buddy?" Sam asked. "The usual?"

"Yep, just a Heineken for me. And send that redhead down there another of whatever she's been drinking."

Darrin placed a twenty on the bar and Sam zipped off to fill the order. He quickly returned, setting the beer down in front Darrin before delivering the redhead her vanilla Stoli and Red Bull. Darrin watched as Sam whispered in her ear and pointed in his direction. He flashed her his winning smile, which she reciprocated with her own flirtatious grin.

"Hey, Darrin," a female voice called from behind him.

Darrin spun around to see who was speaking to him. The petite, blue-eyed platinum blonde took a seat on the barstool next to him. It was Aria, Darrin's former classmate and the woman Raven despised with a passion.

"Aria, hey. How ya been?"

"Pretty good. Staying busy with classes and all. How about you? You still go to Columbia? I haven't seen you on campus since the new semester started."

"No, actually I'm taking a little break. Gonna start back next semester," he lied. Darrin had no plans for the future other than being at Raven's beck and call. As he fell deeper and deeper under her spell, he had come to think of school as a worthless distraction from the only thing in his life that was truly meaningful: Raven. He had completely abandoned his education and his pursuit of an Ivy League degree, as well as his spot on the football team, despite how bad he had initially desired them both.

"How is Melody?" asked Aria. "I haven't seen her either. And how's the baby?"

"The baby...Melody lost the baby." He bowed his head, feigning sorrow as he took on the role of a grieving father. "It really put a strain on me and Mel's relationship, so we're no longer together."

"Oh my God, Darrin. I'm so sorry. I didn't know." Aria rubbed his back to console him.

"It's okay. I'm just taking it one day at a time."

"That's good. Time heals all, right?"

"That's what they say."

"Have you seen Raven lately?" Aria asked, changing the topic to a less touchy one.

"No, not in a while," he lied.

Why is she asking about Raven, Darrin wondered. *They hate each other*.

"Well look, I've gotta get going, but take my number." She jotted her digits onto a napkin and handed it to Darrin. "Call me sometime. We can do more catching up. And don't be afraid to use my number if you're ever feeling down or just need someone to talk to, okay?"

"Okay."

"I'm a great listener," she added with a warm smile.

"Thanks, Aria."

Aria gave Darrin a quick hug before exiting the bar.

Once Aria left, the redhead approached Darrin to introduce herself and thank him for the drink. Her hair was a natural shade of red; more of an orange as opposed to Raven's bright red.

"What do you do for a living," she asked Darrin after exchanging brief introductions.

Darrin paused for a second to think. Some nights he was a screenwriter. On others he decided to be a pilot, or a fireman, or a dentist.

"I'm an engineer," he quickly decided.

"So like, you fix engines and stuff?"

Darrin waited for the laughter he was sure would follow her silly question but he soon realized she was completely serious. The girl was as dumb as a rock.

"Uh, yeah."

Over the next hour the two of them shared small talk and several more drinks. By the time they left the bar to head to Darrin's apartment, he was convinced he'd be doing the world a great service by ridding it of the ditzy, numbskull of a woman.

No sooner than they'd closed the door behind them was she shoving her tongue into his mouth. They got right down to business and began tearing off each other's clothes. Darrin laid her down on the couch and went for her panties, eager to see if the carpet matched the drapes.

It did.

"Nice," he said in approval of the neatly trimmed patch of orange hair.

"Thanks. Now I wanna see yours. Whip it out."

"You want it? Go get it," he said gesturing down to the large bulge in his boxers.

She reached into his underwear and grabbed his meat stick, massaging it up and down before pulling it out.

"*Very* nice," she said before diving down. She inserted his erect penis into her warm mouth – it felt like a little piece of heaven. Darrin allowed his head to fall back onto the couch pillows, enjoying the amazing sensation. *At least she's good for something*, he thought. He was glad he had scored a winner tonight. There was nothing he hated more than a lazy dick suck. But Red was on point. She sucked like a vacuum cleaner, bobbing her head back and forth with enthusiasm. Her mouth stayed good and wet, too; saliva dripped down his shaft and onto his balls. It was sloppy, just like he liked it. She removed her mouth and spit onto his rod while using her hand to jerk him off. He was ready to release, but he felt she deserved one final good fuck before she died. He tapped her on her back and, taking heed to the signal, she laid down on the sofa, spreading her legs wide in anticipation of Darrin's entry. He quickly placed a condom on and slid into her canal.

"Damn, it's nice and tight."

"Feels good, baby?"

"Hell yeah."

Every time Darrin had sex with someone he imagined it was Raven. It had been too long since their last romp and he couldn't wait to feel her again. He closed his eyes and envisioned her body as he stroked away. He had Red's flexible legs pinned back as far as they could go as he pleased her with long, deliberate strokes.

"Raven," he moaned.

"Rachel," she corrected him, not really minding what she thought was a harmless, honest mistake.

He focused on her G-spot, hitting the delicate area with the pressure it needed. Her juices poured out onto the couch, letting Darrin know she was enjoying every minute of it. He swiveled his hips, slowly stirring her overflowing honeypot.

"Damn, you're fucking me like you love me," she said breathlessly.

"I do love you, Raven. You know I do."

This time Rachel was pissed.

"Get the fuck off of me!" she yelled, pushing Darrin. "If you want Raven so bad then go fuck her!"

As she gathered her clothing and began to dress, Darrin went into the kitchen and retrieved a steak knife. It was the only knife he had other than the butter knives, but he figured it would get the job done. He plowed it right into her back while she was bent over stepping into her jeans. Rachel cried out as she tumbled over in pain from the unexpected burn of the serrated edged blade. She attempted to crawl toward the door but Darrin continued stabbing her. Over and over again the knife entered and exited her flesh, causing blood to splatter everywhere. It didn't end until twenty jabs later when her body stopped moving and her breathing ceased.

Darrin shook his head as he looked down at his bloodstained hands and then at the bloody corpse.

"Damn shame," he said. "Waste of a perfectly good piece of ass."

But she had to die. Whatever Raven wanted, Raven got.

VANNA B.

Chapter Five

Darrin was sitting on the edge of his bed with both hands full of bone straight, thin black hair. The Japanese identical twin sisters the hair belonged to were at work below. One entertained his jewels while the other licked his pole up and down.

"Don't be shy, Akari," Darrin coaxed. "Suck that shit."

"I'm Hikaru. She's Akari."

Unfazed by the mix-up, Hikaru took heed to his command. She wrapped her lips around his pipe and sucked so hard her pale cheeks puckered in tightly, giving her a funny, fish-faced appearance. Eager to show off her skills, she moved her mouth further down, taking his entire shaft into her throat without gagging once.

"Shit, girl!" Darrin blurted out, his toes curling from the sensation. She winked at him as she continued sucking and slobbering all over his pulsating cock. Akari took both of his testicles into her mouth, making gurgling noises as she sucked and slurped.

The sisters continued pleasuring Darrin with their mouths until Hikaru got up and lowered herself onto his dick. She slid her slick twat down, and felt it hardening even more inside her. The trio was having too much fun. Hikaru bounced up and down while her sister smacked her butt and giggled. But after several minutes on the back burner, Akari began to get upset. She crossed her arms and poked her bottom lip out, pouting with jealousy. She pushed Hikaru off of Darrin and, straddling his hips, she quickly replaced her sister. Hikaru fell off of the bed and onto the floor, but neither Akari nor Darrin seemed concerned about her spill. Akari was focused on outdoing her sister and Darrin was enjoying the ride, thinking to himself how amazing it was for two women to be completely identical to one another – even in the vagina.

Hikaru crept back onto the bed and sprung at Akari, playfully tackling her to the mattress. Akari giggled and squirmed as her sister pinned her down and tortured her with tickles all over her body. Meanwhile, Darrin was behind them admiring their naked asses stacked atop one another as Hikaru continued her tickle assault. He startled them each with hard smacks to their tight buns before sliding his pipe into Hikaru's slit. He was like a kid at a carnival as he moved from sister to sister, switching between their two tiny pussies every few strokes.

Suddenly the bedroom door opened and in stepped Raven wearing her long, black velvet trench coat. The trio froze and the twins exchanged worried glances, wondering if they were about to have a confrontation with an angry girlfriend.

"Don't stop on account of me," she said, taking a seat in the armchair by the window to watch.

The twins looked back at Darrin with confused and inquisitive expressions.

"Akari and Hikaru, this is Raven – my woman."

Their eyes shifted from him to Raven, who simply rolled her eyes and chuckled in amusement.

"Correction. I am not your woman. I am your owner."

"Well if you're his owner," Hikaru said snidely, still laid on top of her sister, "you mind telling me why he's here fucking us?"

Raven silently rose from her chair and peeked through the blinds at the setting sun. Darrin knew Hikaru had just made a gross mistake but she was none the wiser. Raven walked to bed and hovered over the naked twins, glaring down at them with disgust. Had the sisters known what Darrin knew they would have rose from the vulnerable position and fled immediately. But instead, they foolishly decided to partake in the stare-down with Raven.

"He's fucking you little sluts because I told him to," Raven informed them. "More specifically, because I want your hearts." Akari and Hikaru never saw it coming when Raven pulled a samurai katana sword from inside her coat and removed both of their heads with one clean slice of the 30-inch, hand honed steel blade. Their heads rolled onto the floor while blood spurted from their severed necks like fountains, leaving the bed and carpet soaked and stained.

"I got tired of waiting," Raven shrugged as she kicked Hikaru's body over and sliced her chest open ever so gently, being careful not to puncture her heart. "Guess I got a little hungry and came to see what the hold up was with my dinner."

She removed the heart and held it high, tilting her head back while squeezing it in her fist to allow the still-warm blood to drip into her mouth.

"Only one more left now," said Darrin, beaming with pride at having nearly completed the mission. "And I already know who it will be."

Time to put Aria's number to use, he thought to himself. He was excited about this one. He knew Raven would be impressed when he surprised her by bringing her the heart of the woman she hated most.

Perfectly content at the moment, Raven offered a rare smile back with streams of blood tricking down her chin and neck. Darrin thought she looked   absolutely   beautiful.

Chapter Six

Darrin couldn't wait to get Aria in his bed. She was a gorgeous woman – almost as beautiful as Raven, he thought. She was a small girl, but still had a handful of tits and enough curves to fill out her low-rise jeans nicely. Darrin realized that in all his sexual conquests over the past three months, he had not been with a single blonde. He had always heard that blondes were more fun and he planned to find out for himself before he romanced her, dicked her down, and stole her heart – literally.

He dialed the digits inscribed on the napkin and waited to hear Aria's voice on the other end of the line.

"Hello?" she answered.

Darrin sat silently, waiting for her to repeat herself.

"Helloooo?" Aria said again.

"I'm sorry," he finally said glumly, "I shouldn't have called. I don't want to burden you with my issues."

"Darrin? No, it's totally okay. What's the matter?"

"I'm just more depressed than usual today. Been thinking a lot about Mel and the baby."

"Awww, you wanna talk about it?"

"You sure you want to? I hate to be a downer. But I just can't seem to shake this mood today."

"Of course, Darrin. I told you to call me whenever you need someone to talk to. Have you eaten dinner yet? Let's go out – my treat. It'll do you good to get out of the house."

"Eh, I don't know. My eyes are probably all puffy from crying." Darrin held the phone away and cupped his hand over his mouth to stifle his urge to laugh.

"I'm not taking no for an answer," stated Aria. "We're going to dinner and you're gonna have a good meal and a little fun to take your mind off of it for a while."

"Well, okay," he reluctantly agreed.

"There's a Morrocan place on Wythe Ave. – Café Mogador. It's around the corner from that bar I saw you at the other night. Meet me there in an hour."

Throughout the evening, Darrin kept his act up. If women taking him out and paying for his dinner was the response he'd receive from the made up sob story, he would certainly be telling it more often, he thought. Of course he had to listen to her talk about her mundane life which consisted mainly of classes, caring for her sick mother, and her crappy part-time waitressing job, but it was a small price to pay; he couldn't wait to get Aria back to his apartment where he was sure she'd bless him with some good pity pussy.

After dinner they made their way back to his place and soon started down the right path with kissing, rubbing, and heavy petting. Things were heating up. But when Darrin tried to unbutton her pants, Aria stopped him.

"What's wrong?" he asked, disappointed and irked.

"It's that time of the month."

For Darrin, that wasn't a good enough excuse. "So? I don't care about that."

Aria got up from the couch with a sigh and went for her jacket and purse. "I should be going. I've got class in the morning."

"You sure you don't want to stay?" Darrin asked, desperately. "If you leave me alone I might get depressed all over again." He put on the saddest expression he could muster, complete with the frown and puppy dog eyes.

Aria laughed. "I see what you're doing, Darrin. You do know that, right? You thought you were gonna get me to feel all sad and sorry for you and give up the ass. Well, I hate to break it to you, but you've got the wrong one."

Darrin didn't appreciate being patronized. "No," he said, reaching under the couch cushion, "*You* got the wrong one, bitch!"

He swung the knife at Aria, but she jumped back, dodging the blade. To Darrin's surprise, instead of running toward the door, Aria went for the counterattack. She rushed back at him, kicking him square in the loins.

"Ughhhh!" he shouted in agony as he doubled over, clutching his privates. The intense pain shooting from his testicles to his stomach left him crippled. Aria followed up with a sharp elbow to the back of Darrin's neck that sent him straight down to the ground. She kicked the knife across the room before grabbing Darrin's arm and twisting it behind his back.

"Where's Raven?!" she demanded, putting so much pressure on his arm, he thought it would snap at any moment.

"Why the fuck do you wanna know?" he spat through clenched teeth.

"Where is she?!" She pushed harder on his arm as she dug her knee into his spine. Darrin winced and cried out from the pain.

"Go to Hell!" He refused to give up Raven's location, no matter what. The threat of bodily harm and even death was nothing compared to his undying love for her.

"That's okay," said Aria. "I don't need you to tell me."

Aria wanted badly to break his arm right then and there. She could have easily done so, as she had done many times before. But sending him to the hospital would only have wasted time and caused a delay in her plans. So she decided stamping the heel of her boot into his lumbar vertebrae would have to do for now. It would hurt like hell for weeks and would make practically everything he did painful. Darrin's anguished screams filled the small apartment as her sole met his back.

"That's for the innocent child you helped slaughter," she informed him. "How could you? Your own flesh and blood. And poor Melody." Aria wiped a lone tear that had formed in the corner of her eye before getting up and putting on her jacket. She opened the door to leave and turned back to take one last look at Darrin, who was still on the floor shouting obscenities at her as he held onto his aching back.

"There's a special place in Hell waiting just for you. Too bad I can't be the one to send you there."

With that, Aria swung her shoulder bag over her arm, and walked out, slamming the door behind her.

VANNA B.

Chapter Seven

Darrin crept up a dark alley wallowing in disappointment. He had wanted the thirteenth victim to be someone meaningful. Bringing Raven Aria's heart would have pleased her immensely. But he had failed miserably and now he would have to settle for a random person off the street; a nobody as worthless to Raven as she most likely was to the rest of the world.

Darrin was confused. He now knew that Aria intended to use him to get to Raven – but why? Furthermore, how did she know about the baby? The questions continued to circle in his brain.

Eager to get the final kill over with and bring the heart to Raven, Darrin stationed himself at the top of the alley, just where it let out into a residential street. He crouched in the shadows, waiting for a suitable victim to come along.

The first woman who passed by would have made an excellent target if she hadn't been walking her 140-pound Rottweiler. Darrin was not about to risk becoming the large and potentially vicious dog's dinner. He would just have to be patient and wait for someone else to walk by.

The next woman that came along was a jogger. The headphones blaring in her ears might have made it easy to sneak up on her if she had not been moving so fast. She zipped right by the alley before Darrin even had a chance to pursue her.

Finally the misfortunate one, a heavyset woman who appeared to be in her early thirties, came treading along. She wore a business suit with gray Nike Air Maxes and she looked exhausted. Darrin imagined she must have been on her way home after working overtime at her boring office job where she spent her day staring at a computer screen in her tiny cubicle. In one hand she carried a black leather briefcase; the other gripped the straps of a canvas tote that might have contained the heels she wore all day and happily traded for her sneakers before heading home.

This will be easy, he thought to himself. *Her big ass will get winded fast, plus everyone knows "the bigger they are, the harder they fall."* Darrin planned on using her weight to his advantage, minimizing the work he'd have to do.

As soon as the woman reached the alley, Darrin leapt out from the darkness, attacking her from behind. Startled, the woman jumped and dropped her belongings. Not wanting to give her an opportunity to scream, he forced his hand over her mouth and began trying to drag her into the alley where she'd be out of view to anyone who may have come along. She wasn't going down without a fight, though. The woman swung her arms about wildly, her heavy fists striking Darrin with several uncoordinated punches. He had no choice but to remove his hand from over her mouth to wrap both arms around her in a bear hug hold. As soon as he did, she screamed out as loud as she could.

"HELLLLLP!!!"

The woman bucked, putting up quite a struggle as Darrin continued pulling her into the shadows. He had underestimated her. Her size proved to be more of an asset than a weakness, and she wasn't half as winded as he was. The strain she was putting on his body, coupled with his previous injury courtesy of Aria, had his back aching terribly. But with her arms pinned down, it was easier for Darrin to maneuver the large woman into the alleyway. Once concealed by its darkness, he knew he only had a split second to grab his knife. Holding the woman with one hand would allow the possibility of her overpowering him and escaping. But he had to shut her up before someone realized what was happening and either called the police or tried to intervene.

"Somebody help me!" she yelled. "I'm being attacked!"

As fast as he could, he snatched the knife from his back pocket and forcefully thrust it up under her chin. Inside her open mouth he could see the jagged blade cut through her tongue and puncture the roof of her mouth. This was enough to shut her up and send her tumbling to the ground clutching he gushing entry wound. Darrin hurriedly sliced the woman's chest wide open and snatched her beating heart right out of its cavity. Then he ran off into the night, leaving the mutilated corpse behind.

Chapter Eight

Tired, sore, and out of breath, Darrin staggered into the cathedral, rubbing his lower back with one hand and carrying the still-warm heart in the other.

"What happened to you?" Raven inquired, reaching out to take her dinner into her hands. "Number thirteen put up a fight? You're limping in here holding your back like an old ass man."

"I saw Aria. She must be looking for you. She asked me where you were."

"What?! Aria?" Raven paused from devouring the heart and her face took on an expression Darrin had never before seen on it – a look of fear. "You didn't tell her where I am, did you?

"No."

Raven exhaled in relief before contorting her face into an angry scowl and yelling, "Why didn't you kill her, you fucking idiot?!"

"I tried! I wanted to surprise you by bringing you her heart because I know how much you hate her. She's a good fighter, though. She must have taken some self defense classes or something." Darrin rubbed his aching back again.

"No, you fool," Raven said as she polished off the last of the thirteenth heart, completing her yearly feast. "She's a vigilante demon hunter. Thinks she's goddamn Van Helsing or some shit. I don't know where the bitch came from, but she's been on my ass for the last couple of years. So anyway, where'd you see her?"

"I saw her at a bar near my apartment a few days ago. She took me to dinner tonight and I brought her back to my apartment to try—"

"Your apartment?! You let her know where you live?! How fucking stupid can you be? She could have—"

"Followed you here." The voice completing Raven's sentence did not belong to Darrin. Raven carefully backed away as Aria stepped out of the shadows holding a silver recurve bow with an arrow already resting on the nock. To the naked eye, the arrow appeared to be nothing more than a fancy replica fashioned from glass. But upon further examination one could see the arrow stretching the tightly pulled bowstring was actually a custom-made, arrow-shaped glass vial. There were five more identical to it situated inside the leather arrow quiver strapped to her back. Each arrowhead was sharpened until its point was as thin and sharp as a needle. And each of the arrows was filled with holy water, blessed by the Pope himself in St. Peter's Basillica.

Darrin sprung up, preparing to defend Raven, but Aria aimed the arrow square between his eyes. Aria watched them fill with fear as he weak-heartedly retreated. In a flash, Raven vanished into thin air, leaving Darrin's eyes scouring the sanctuary in astonishment. Aria didn't seem too concerned, though. She maintained an air of confidence. Seconds after her disappearing act Raven reappeared, bouncing off of the door with a force that sent her flying across the room. She slammed into the opposite wall before finally falling to the floor below. Rather than running to her aid, Darrin sat frozen, bewildered at how the invisible force had launched her body that far.

"Oh, I'm sorry," Aria sang, inching toward Raven. "I forgot to mention that little ward I placed on the exits. No teleporting for you."

Raven was cornered with nowhere to run. She closed her eyes and began babbling words in a foreign tongue. Aria undoubtedly recognized the ancient dialect as Aramaic.

"Trying to cast a spell on me, huh?" she asked, refocusing the arrow's aim on its intended target as Raven snatched the amulet from her neck and enclosed it in her fist behind her back. When she opened her hand, the amulet was gone. She had discretely made it vanish into thin air.

"Not today, bitch," Aria smirked as she released the arrow, sending it hurling directly at Raven. The glass arrow pierced through her chest, puncturing her heart and shattering inside of it, allowing the holy water to seep into the body her demonic spirit had inhabited for the past decade. Raven shrieked as she burst into flames and the flesh was burned from her bones.

"Noooooo!" Darrin screamed, running to her burning body. He threw his coat on top of her, using the heavy leather bomber to douse the flames. It was too late, though. By the time the fire was quelled, there was nothing left of Raven but an unidentifiable smoking corpse and the stench of burnt meat. Distraught, Darrin collapsed helplessly to the floor. Overcome with grief from the tragic loss of his love, all he could do was cry hysterically. Suddenly his grief was replaced with rage. His eyes scanned the room for Aria but she was gone.

"I have to kill her," he said aloud, clenching his fists. "I should've killed her when I had the chance! Now because of me, Raven is dead!"

And just like that his anger had morphed back into despair. Darrin continued his frantic crying episode until he decided he simply could not go on any more. What was the point? There was no way he could possibly live without his beloved Raven. He searched the sanctuary for something to aid him in his suicide – a rope, a knife, or some other sharp object – but all he found was the amulet Raven wore around her neck daily. He picked it up and enclosed it in his hand, bringing it close to his heart. Again, he fell to his knees, and like an out-of-control child having a temper tantrum, he banged his head against the wooden slats of the floor as hard as he could. Over and over, he slammed his dome to the floor, hoping for a death-inducing brain hemorrhage. All he did, however, was knock himself out cold.

While he lay unconscious, Raven came to Darrin in a lucid dream. She sat down on the floor beside him and rested his head in her lap.

"My dear Darrin, don't be sad." She spoke to him in a delicate and comforting tone that ensured him he was dreaming. She gently stroked his cheek and kissed each of his parted lips. Raven ran her fingertips over Darrin's chest, touching him more softly than she ever had in reality. Her mouth slowly moved over his body, planting wet kisses wherever it traveled. He felt her breath on his skin; it was like the gentle flutter of butterfly wings. Then he found himself inside her. It was as fantastic as it had always been. But this time it was different. She was not the usual rough, raunchy Raven. She was tender…sweet…loving, even. Yes, she was making love to him for the first time ever. Although he realized he was dreaming, it seemed so vivid and real. He could see her face, feel her body, and hear her voice as clear as day.

"I may not be here with you right now, Darrin, but we can be together once again. If you follow my instructions and do exactly as I say, we can be together forever."

Darrin stared into her piercing almond-shaped brown eyes, soaking in her every word. If what she was saying was true – if there was a way for them to be together – he would do whatever was necessary to make it happen.

"I need a human body. A vessel I can resurrect in," she continued. "Do not kill them;

bring them here alive. Once you have the body, there are three things you must do. The first is to place the amulet around their neck. Next, lay them in the center of the pentagram. And finally, you recite these words: Aael khayat d'shiada ealmanaya aesuoksea. Go now. The sooner you do this the sooner I'll return to you."

Darrin regained consciousness with a powerful orgasm rippling through his body. There was no doubt in his mind that Raven had purposely entered his dream. It had not been merely a figment of his imagination. It was as real as the night was dark. Disregarding his aching head and back, he coaxed himself up off of the floor and out into the New York streets. He had no time to waste. Every minute that passed was another moment without Raven. He could not rest until she was once again by his side.

ChaPteR NiNe

Darrin bounded down the concrete steps of the church with the intention of snatching up whatever unlucky pedestrian he happened to see first. He knew he couldn't go too far since he'd have to bring the entire person back with him alive and in one piece, so instead he'd allow his victim to come to him. He sat nonchalantly on the steps, waiting for someone to pass by. Within moments, someone happened along. The freakishly thin forty-something woman ambled his way, her high-heeled boots clacking against the cement as she made her best attempt at swaying her bony hips enticingly. Despite the chilly fall night, she donned a short mini-skirt and a cropped top under her open jacket, exposing her stick-thin legs, caved in stomach, and visible ribcage.

Darrin walked right up to the woman without saying a word. She must have mistaken Darrin for homeless after noticing him camped out on the cathedral stairs, because when she saw him approaching she said, "I don't think so, buddy. I don't do bums and I don't work for change."

"Shut up, bitch," Darrin said before slugging the woman with a right hook, instantly knocking her unconscious. Her eyes crossed as her legs went limp and her frail body dropped to the cold cement.

Darrin easily hoisted the pile of bones over his shoulder and carried her inside the church, laying her in the middle of the pentagram as Raven had instructed. He took the amulet from his pocket and placed it around the hooker's neck before stepping out of the five-sided marking.

"Okay, here we go," he said taking a final deep breath before uttering the Aramaic phrase. "Aael khayat d'shiada ealmanaya aesuoksea."

Darrin's heart raced with excitement as he anticipated Raven's return. He didn't know whether to expect sparks, smoke, or for the body to float up into the air and levitate as he stood watching, but he was anxiously awaiting whatever was about to happen. He carefully observed the body, waiting for some sign of life; fluttering of the eyes, a gasp for breath, twitching – something. But there was nothing. Darrin was sure he had done everything Raven had said to do. Had he pronounced one of the words wrong? He recited the phrase again, this time louder.

"Aael khayat d'shiada ealmanaya aesuoksea!"

Nothing. He shook the body, hoping Raven was in there somewhere. Again, nothing. Darrin was crushed. The resurrection was a failure. *The whole thing was a fluke*, he thought to himself, wondering if he had knocked his brain loose while banging his head on the floor, or if he was just that deep in denial about Raven's death he actually believed he could bring her back. Feeling altogether depressed and defeated, Darrin sulked toward the door to leave Raven behind forever.

Once again in tears, he kneeled down beside the badly burnt corpse and grasped one of its crisped hands, but it only crumbled to ashes in his palm. Darrin kissed her charred forehead one last time.

"I will love you forever, Raven," he whispered, taking a final look at her. "Goodbye."

"What do ya mean goodbye? I'm just getting started."

Darrin's face lit up with sheer joy as he watched the body of the prostitute rise from the floor and sassily throw a hand on its bony hip. Raven was back.

"Raven!!!" Darrin ran to her and hoisted her up in the air, twirling her around with glee.

"Yep, in the flesh," she joked. "Can you put me down now?"

Darrin gently placed her feet back on the floor before wiping the tears of joy from his face.

"You died on me, Raven; you actually died. I thought you were immortal. Wasn't that the whole point of eating the hearts?"

"No, you idiot. The hearts are for eternal life. That just means I can continue to live in human form no matter how old I get. Whatever body I inhibit will never die of old age. That doesn't mean I can't be killed. You couldn't have found a better body than this, though?" she asked, looking down at the emaciated bag of bones. "Ugh, this bitch needed a cheeseburger bad. And these clothes. She should've switched professions if she couldn't afford anything better than this with her whoring income. Luckily, I can fix it."

Raven closed her eyes and her entire body began to vibrate. Her skin softened and turned visibly malleable as she continued to shake faster and faster, soon becoming nothing but a blur. Darrin watched as Raven shape-shifted right before his eyes, morphing back into her previous body form, complete with long bright red hair, killer curves, and tattoos.

"There's my Raven!" Darrin exclaimed. "You know I still would have loved you in the old street walker's body, but this one...mmmm, this one is IT!"

"Can't argue with you there," she shrugged. "I'm one sexy ass bitch!" Darrin and Raven shared a quick laugh.

"Now I've got to find something more suitable to wear."

Just then the alarm on Darrin's watch sounded, letting him know it was 12:00 midnight.

"Happy birthday, Raven!"

"Ah yes, it's great to see another wicked year on this wretched earth! Thanks for your help, Darrin but it's time for us to part ways. You won't be seeing me anymore."

"What, are you joking?" Darrin asked, confused. His face fell once again as his excitement was drained.

"Nope, not at all. You've served your purpose. But it's out with the old and in with the new. I'm celebrating a new year here. I'm in a new body. The only thing that's not new is you."

"You can't leave me, Raven. Please! I love you!"

"As do all of those who came before you."

"You told me we'd be together forever!"

"Silly rabbit, that was just a dream," she laughed. "Okay, no really…I lied."

"But why? Why would you do this to me."

"Oh, Darrin. That's just way I do things. I use men until I get tired of them and then I discard them like the trash that they are. Plus, that Aria situation was an epic fuck up on your part. You proved to me just how dim-witted and worthless you truly are. Did you actually think I'd keep you around after that shit? I need her dead and you've proven to me you're incapable of pulling that off."

Having gone from feeling hopeless over Raven's death to ecstatic about her resurrection and now desperately distraught he was losing her again, Darrin was on an emotional rollercoaster. He graveled on his knees before her, holding onto her leg as he begged and cried shamelessly.

"Please don't leave me, Raven! What will I do without you?"

"That's your problem. Now beat it. I don't ever want to see your face again."

VANNA B.

Chapter Ten

For the next three days, Darrin stayed cooped up in his apartment with all the blinds tightly closed. He didn't eat and he barely slept. He didn't watch TV. He didn't shower. In fact, he didn't leave the bed at all – not even to use the bathroom. He spent most of his time curled up under the covers in a fetal position. The only activity he partook in was crying, often writhing about as if experiencing corporeal pain. He planned to just lie there in his own urine and feces until he died of starvation or dehydration, whichever occurred first. He felt that his heart was physically broken. It no longer beat the same. The way it pumped blood through his body was simply inadequate. A piece of it was no longer there.

A knock at his door woke him up from a restless slumber. He ignored it. It was probably just the landlord looking for the rent. Then a thought crept into his mind: What if was Raven? What if she changed her mind? What if she needed him? He couldn't risk it. Darrin mustered every bit of his remaining energy to climb out of bed and trot to the door. As he reached for the doorknob, his heart thumped with excitement at the possibility that Raven could be standing on the other side of the door. Though he hadn't prayed in over a year, he neither thought twice nor found any irony in saying a quick silent prayer asking God to bring the diabolical demon temptress back to him – his desperation had caused him to do much worse.

Darrin braced himself as he pulled the door open. His face and posture instantly drooped with disappointment and dismay. The unexpected visitor was not who he had hoped, and the last person he expected.

"Melody?"

VANNA B.

Chapter One

Darrin couldn't believe he was standing face to face with Melody. He never in his wildest dream would have imagined he'd see her again, but there she was, standing in the doorway of the apartment they once shared. They stood there glaring at one another in silence, each studying the other's expression. Darrin's was one of complete shock while Melody's face bore the unmistakable look of pure hatred. After several moments, Darrin started to push the door closed, but Melody prevented it by lodging her foot in the door. Given Darren's weakened state, she easily pushed the door open and forced her way inside. That is when the putrid stench of urine and feces hit her.

"Fuck!" she yelled, holding her hand up to her nose in attempt to keep the foul odor out of her nostrils.

"Since when do you curse?" Darrin asked uninterestedly, as he turned and moped back to his deathbed. The entire back of his blue sweatpants had turned a nasty shade of brown; the seat of them sagged, weighed down with pounds of his own excrement. Melody was utterly disgusted and wanted badly to get as far away as possible from the awful smell. Nevertheless, she found herself following him into the bedroom out of sheer

121

curiosity. There the stench was even worse. Darrin climbed back onto his filthy mattress, and curled up right on top of the large wet stain that matched the one on his soiled pants. Melody could hold her lunch no more. She bent over in the corner, releasing all the contents of her stomach onto the carpet.

"Fucking disgusting," she sneered, wiping her mouth with her coat sleeve. "You don't even realize what she's done to you."

Darrin ignored her comments. His back was turned to her and he had buried his head under a pillow.

"You know, I came here to kill you." Melody removed the gun from her waistband. She held it in her palm and stroked its shiny black finish. After examining the instrument of death for a moment, she placed it back in her pants and pulled her jacket down over it.

"I'm not going to do it, though. There's no point in even wasting the bullet. From what I can see you're already living in Hell. Just look at yourself. You're literally living in shit. And your face…it looks like you've aged ten years. She's drained your life force. She's a succubus, Darrin; that's what they do. I looked it up on the Internet and it all makes so much sense now. Every time you fucked that bitch, she took a little piece of your soul; drained you for more and more of it each time, and now, there's hardly anything left. I guess you thought you were just getting your rocks off…trying to get a quick nut…just being a man. Well right from the very first time you stuck your dick in her she was able to control you. She made you do those horrible things. I realize that now. But if you think I feel one single iota of sympathy for you, you're wrong."

The rage that had been rising up inside of Melody finally reached the surface and began to boil over.

"YOU succumbed to temptation," she yelled, pointing her finger at him, "and YOU deserved everything that came to you because YOU brought it on your fucking self!"

"You're weak!" she screamed with tears pouring from her eyes. "You're pathetic! I can't believe I loved you and wanted to marry you."

Darrin continued to ignore Melody as she shouted over him, crying hysterically and releasing what she'd been keeping pent up for far too long.

"You ruined my life and took away the best thing that ever happened to me! I carried her for nine months only to have her ripped from my womb! I never even got a chance to see her face or watch her sleep. Her cries…I never got to hear them. I never got to hold my baby girl in my arms…"

Melody's voice trailed off and she fell silent as she held her arms up rocking an imaginary baby. Everything that had happened had taken a major toll on her. She spent much of her time angry and crying and she was well aware that her mental state had seriously deteriorated.

"No!" she shot at Darrin once the rage returned. "I'm *not* going to end your suffering. I'm going to let you live out the rest of your miserable, worthless life in your own personal Hell. And then, when you die, you can go to Hell again, you son-of-a-bitch!"

Melody stormed out of the stinking apartment and bounded down the stairs. Back onto the cold Brooklyn streets it was for her. She had returned to New York to exact her revenge on the two individuals responsible for her misery. Killing Darrin would have been easy. Killing Raven, not so much. Melody knew there was a great chance the outcome of that face-off would not be in her favor. The way she saw it, though, she had nothing to live for anyway.

Chapter Two

The way Melody entered the old cathedral was nothing like the way she entered it the first time. She was a scared, timid girl then. This time she boldly walked through the doors, gun drawn and ready to kill. She had dreamt of the moment she would see Raven again. How she longed to make her swallow an entire clip full of bullets. She couldn't wait to watch Raven's head explode like a summer melon when she blasted her brains out. She hoped killing her would help take some of the pain away and give her closure. Either way, she would enjoy every second of her revenge.

The church appeared to be empty. It was dark, as it always was, but Melody came prepared with a flashlight. She clicked it on and, holding the gun in one hand and the flashlight in the other, she moved it around the sanctuary using its light to guide her path.

Suddenly Melody stopped dead in her tracks. She could have sworn she'd heard something behind her. She whipped around, allowing the flashlight's ray to illuminate the area. She saw nothing and, satisfied that it was only the settling of the old building, she continued on. She had barely gotten six feet away when she heard another noise. Again, she turned to scan the area around her. That is when she noticed a door. She heard movement for the third time and this time she was sure it was coming from behind that door. Melody clicked the flashlight off and carefully crept over to the door as quietly as she possibly could. Aiming at the door, she held her finger in place on the trigger, ready to face Raven once and for all. She slowly reached for the doorknob and, on the count of three, quickly yanked it open. As soon as the door opened someone sprang at her from behind it. Her gut told her it was Raven. Melody squeezed the trigger and the gunshot echoed in the huge building as she was tackled to the ground. The gun flew out of her hand, clanking to the floor several feet away before sliding further into the darkness.

"You fucking bitch, I'm gonna kill you for what you did to my baby!" Melody growled as she kicked and struggled to break free. Her attacker had her pinned down on the floor by her wrists and was pressing every pound of their body weight on top of her.

"Your baby?" the assailant asked, loosening her hold. "Melody, is that you?"

Once free, Melody retrieved her flashlight and turned it on, shining it on the face of the person she thought was Raven, but obviously wasn't. The piercing crystal blue eyes squinted in the bright light.

"Aria?" Melody had to blink to make sure it was really her. "What the fuck are you doing here?"

"No, what are *you* doing here?"

"I'm looking for Raven," she replied as she picked her gun up from the floor.

Aria had to laugh. "You came to kill Raven…with a gun?"

"Didn't realize you two were friends now. Where is the bitch?"

"Whoa, me and Raven are not friends."

"Then what are you doing here?"

"I'm looking for her the same as you are."

"I'm confused."

"Well that's obvious," Aria laughed. "If you think you're going to kill Raven with that," she said, pointing to the gun, "you're more than confused. You're delusional."

Aria drove Melody back to her apartment to fill her in. Neither of them had eaten so they talked over a quick dinner of pizza and wings.

"About Raven," Aria began, "You know that she's more than just a witch, right?"

"Yeah, a succubus."

"Right. A succubus is a demon. And killing a demon is much more complicated than killing a human."

"How do you know about killing demons?" Melody inquired.

"I'm a hunter."

"A hunter?"

"Yes, a demon hunter."

Melody laughed. "How'd you get into that line of work? Did you just wake up one morning and decide you wanted to kill demons?"

"Not at all. The ability to sense them is like a sixth sense. It's an extremely rare trait that's strictly hereditary. Oddly enough, it's considered a gift, so if you have it you're kind of obligated to use it. My mom wouldn't have had it any other way, anyhow. I inherited my ability from her. She was a hunter."

"Before she got sick?"

"Yes. Well, before she got hurt. A few weeks back we were in Long Island and caught the scent of a demon. We tracked it down and it turned out to be Raven. We went in for the kill but since it wasn't a planned attack we had limited weaponry on us. My mom barely escaped with her life. In the hospital, she started getting better, but then her condition really started to regress. The doctors said she wouldn't have long but I wasn't trying to hear that...they don't know everything. After that I moved her in here with me. I know I can care for her better than they can. So I've just been nursing her back to health, trying to get her back on her feet again. She'll get there soon, though, ya know? Soon..."

Aria turned her back to Melody attempting to hide the fact that she was on the verge of tears. She stood at kitchen door looking out into the living room where her mother was sleeping. Melody could tell she was getting emotional.

"It's getting late," Melody said. "You want to finish this conversation tomorrow? I'll be in the city for a while. I came back for a reason and I'm

128

not leaving until I accomplish what I came here to do. I'm gonna head back to my hotel and get some rest."

"Look, I know you hate her – so do I – but you're going to have to give up this mission of yours. You're in way over your head. You're gonna get yourself killed."

"Then so be it! When she ripped my daughter from me I was unconscious – completely out of it. I didn't know what was going on and just laid there while it happened. I couldn't fight for her innocent life or do anything to stop it. The least I can do is try to avenge her death. She deserves that much from her mother."

When the tears welled up in Melody's eyes she made no attempt to hold them back. She couldn't have if she tried. She had become accustomed to crying her eyes out. She was used to being sad. For her, it wasn't something she felt she needed to hide. It was a permanent state of emotion.

"Thanks for the dinner," Melody said as she wiped her eyes on her sleeve and walked toward the door.

"I'll help you get your revenge." Aria's words stopped Melody in her tracks. Now she was speaking her language. She didn't want to hear any more about the possibility of her getting killed. That meant nothing to her. All she cared about was seeing Raven's head roll.

"I think you should stay here. I can protect you. Raven won't return to the church because I've already found her there once. But there's no telling who she might have had watching the place."

"Why did you go back there then?"

"A few days ago I killed her and thought she was finally dead for good. Then I sensed that she was alive. She's found another vessel and is still walking among us. I was hoping to turn up a clue as to where she might have gone. No such luck, though."

"How will we find her?"

"You just leave that up to me. That's what I do."

Chapter Three

Melody was relieved that Aria had extended the offer for her to crash at her apartment. She was exhausted and the last thing she felt like doing was taking the subway back to Manhattan. Staying at Aria's was a much better alternative, even if she did have to share Aria's bed with her.

Since Aria had her mother set up in the living room, she'd had to put her couch in storage to make room for the hospital bed. She had offered to camp out on the floor and let Melody have the bed but Melody saw no need for it. Her bed was a queen size and there was plenty of room for both of them. Halfway through the night, though, Aria started to regret her decision. Melody tossed and turned all night long.

"No! Noooooo!" she had yelled out at one point, obviously in the midst of a nightmare. "Stop it! Please, don't do it. Noooooo!"

Aria had to put on her headphones to block out Melody's tormented cries.

When morning came the next day, Aria didn't mention the night screams or bother asking Melody about her dream. And it was a good thing. Melody had no interest in discussing it. All she wanted to do was get right down to business and figure out how they were going to get rid of Raven. She went into the kitchen and waited while Aria finished feeding her mother. Once she was done, she came in and filled two bowls with the cinnamon raisin oatmeal she had prepared for breakfast. Aria set one of the bowls in front of Melody before taking her seat across the table.

"So how do we kill the bitch?" Melody asked as soon as Aria was seated.

"That's what we have to figure out," Aria replied before digging into her oatmeal. "We need a foolproof plan. Killing her for good isn't easy. I've killed her several times before. The problem is I've never destroyed the amulet."

"What amulet?"

"That big black stone she always wears around her neck," said Aria, with a mouthful of food. "That's not just some pretty jewel. It contains her soul."

"Didn't know demons had souls."

"Soul, spirit…whatever you want to call it. That amulet is the key to killing her permanently. We kill the body, destroy the amulet, and she's gone for good."

"Seems simple enough."

"It's not. She's crafty, she's strong, and she'll protect the amulet at all costs. Every time I've killed whatever body she was inhabiting, she's been able to keep the amulet in tact. After that she was resurrected and was able to come back to take over another human body."

"What about when she takes it off? If we can get close somehow we can swap the real amulet for a fake. Then she won't even know it's gone."

"Impossible. I've only ever seen her remove it in the seconds before death to keep it from being destroyed, and even then, she often casts a spell to make it vanish."

"Well what if she *has* to take it off? Like if she's arrested and the police make her remove it."

"Come on, do you really think Raven will allow herself to be arrested?"

"I guess not," Melody sighed.

She and Aria continued eating in silence until several minutes later when Aria started choking on her food. She jumped up from her chair, knocking her bowl onto the floor as she went into a coughing fit.

"Are you okay?" Melody asked with genuine concern.

Aria nodded yes as she continued coughing and pounding her fist on her chest.

Melody quickly filled up a glass of water and handed it to Aria who, despite the choking episode, was smiling. After downing the last drop of water and wiping her watery eyes, Aria's flushed face still displayed the silly grin.

"I've got it!" she excitedly announced, as soon as she was able to speak again. "I know how we can kill her!"

"How?" Melody asked, her eyes widening as she began to feel the excitement.

"Every November there's this huge event called The Festival of Black Magic. It's held in a different city each year and we are in luck because this year it's being held overseas! London to be exact."

"Annnd what's so good about it being abroad?" asked a confused Melody.

"She can't teleport over large bodies of water!" Aria giddily responded. "She'll have no choice but to catch a flight."

"I'm sorry, I still don't see how that benefits us."

"You were on to something with what you said about switching the amulet when she takes it off. Who besides the police can force people to remove their jewelry?"

"Stick-up kids?"

"Well, yeah, but who else?"

Melody shrugged her shoulders. She was clueless and getting annoyed.

"Enough of the games," she snapped at Aria. "Would you just fucking tell me already?"

"Ughhh, the TSA, Mel! When she goes through airport security, she'll have to take the amulet off!"

Melody was irked. That was her foolproof plan? The idea she almost died choking on her breakfast over?

"That might not even work, Aria. They don't always make you take all your jewelry off. And how are we supposed to switch it? Don't you think she'll be watching the damn thing like a hawk? And if she even sees us—"

"You're not thinking right. Let me break it down for you…"

And with that, Aria pulled her chair closer, leaned over the table, and began to lay out her brilliant scheme.

VANNA B.

Chapter Four

"Mom, I have someone I want you to meet," Aria said as she led Melody by the hand over to her mother's bedside. Melody hated being around sickly, dying people. It was depressing. And over the past three-and-a-half months she had already experienced enough depression to last her the rest of her life. Although she didn't really feel up to meeting Aria's mom, Melody was not about to be rude and disrespect Aria in her own home. She was grateful for her opening her doors to her and especially for agreeing to partner up with her to take Raven down. The least she could do is smile through the forced introduction.

"This is Melody," said Aria, placing Melody's hand into her mother's. The ill woman's palms were cold and clammy. Her skin was rough, from engaging in many battles over the years, Melody supposed. She looked into the woman's striking blue eyes. They were the same icy hue as Aria's and although they were kind, they looked like they had seen a lot.

"So nice to meet you, ma'am," Melody said. The woman offered a weak half smile and it was then that Melody noticed just how much Aria favored her. Aria's mom gave Melody's hand a gentle squeeze. She attempted to speak but could only manage a faint inaudible whisper. Aria moved her ear next to her mother's lips so she could hear her.

"She said you're a good person – very special – and that your soul is pure. She also said your heart is full of sorrow right now, but that you will learn to love again."

The woman nodded her confirmation.

"She can read people," Aria explained. "The way she can sense evil spirits, she can also sense good ones."

Melody forced an awkward smile, skeptical about the woman's words.

* * * * *

Later that day Aria and Melody parked at Laguardia Airport and walked inside.

"All flights to London leave from either Terminal B or C. She'll be going through security here," Aria said as they strolled into the bustling security area. They needed to have a good view of the metal detectors and X-ray machines, so once they found a suitable spot next to the winding line of travelers, they stopped. The two women appeared to be carrying on a casual conversation but they were actually carefully observing; monitoring the TSA employees as they searched flight passengers and their carry-on luggage.

"I think I've found our guy," said Aria, smiling. "The tall dude with the salt and pepper low-cut and mustache. Look how he's bossing all the workers around. He's the one calling the shots."

"Yeah, he's definitely in charge," Melody agreed. "He looks mean, though. How am I gonna pique his interest?"

"Come on, are you for real? You're beautiful! What man wouldn't be interested in you?"

"You think I'm beautiful?" asked Melody, with a shy smile. She was blushing.

"I've always thought so, ever since I first saw you," Aria earnestly admitted.

The women shared an awkward moment of silence before Aria focused back on the business at hand.

"We're getting off topic," she reminded Melody.

"Right, right. What if he's married or something?"

"Like being married has ever stopped a man from falling for the charms of a gorgeous woman."

Aria had a point. Most men shared a weakness for young, pretty women. And Melody was going to make every attempt to take advantage of that weakness. In order for their plan to work, they needed him.

* * * * *

That night Melody tossed and turned more than usual. Again, the sudden outbursts of screams

139

filled the otherwise quiet apartment. They were so loud, Aria was afraid they would wake her mother, even with the bedroom door closed. She didn't want to wake Melody but she had to do something or else no one else would get any sleep. She snuggled up behind Melody and wrapped her arm around her. She held her close and then something remarkable happened. The screaming came to an abrupt halt. The restlessness stopped. For the first time in months, Melody had a sound night's sleep.

Chapter Five

The next day Melody suited up for the task at hand, making sure to dress the part. She hadn't packed any sexy clothing for her trip – not that she owned a lot of it to begin with. Luckily, she and Aria wore the same size.

Aria was deep in her closet, rummaging through clothing and tossing suitable items onto the bed. A denim skirt landed in Melody's lap; she immediately shook her head in protest when she saw how short it was.

"No way. You're trying to make me look like a stripper!"

"It's not that short, Mel. Don't be scared to show some leg. Remember, the goal here is *sexy*."

Melody huffed and reluctantly slid her jeans off. She turned her back to Aria but she could feel her eyes on her body as she undressed. She quickly slid the small skirt on. It was way too tight, Melody thought.

"Perfect!" sang Aria. "Yup, he'll definitely want to fuck you."

"What?! You didn't say anything about fucking anyone!"

"Because it goes without saying. How else do you think you're going to persuade him?"

"Why me, though? I'm practically a virgin. Why can't you do it?"

"Because I can't. But don't worry about it. It'll be easy. All you really have to do is lay there and moan like you're enjoying it...I guess."

"What do you mean you guess? Don't tell me you're a virgin too?"

"Well actually, I'm a lesbian. I don't do men."

"Seriously?" Melody asked, intrigued.

"Yup. That's why it has to be you."

"So I'm supposed to take lessons on sexing a man from a goddamn lesbian? Boy am I fucked – no pun intended."

"Shut up," Aria chuckled.

She held open a white button-up collared blouse for Melody to slip into and Melody began fastening the buttons.

"Here, let me," said Aria, grabbing both sides of the shirt at the bottom. She pulled them tightly and tied them into a cute bow that sat right above Melody's navel. Then she undid the first couple of buttons, allowing for a necessary display of cleavage. She focused on her task, doing her best not to stare at Melody's body, but still she couldn't help but admire her small, firm breasts hugged by the nude lace push-up bra. She was glad when she was finished. The last thing she wanted was to make Melody uncomfortable. She wasn't sure how she'd feel about her now that she was aware of her sexual orientation.

"Can you fit an eight in shoes?" Aria asked, heading back to the closet.

"I'm a seven-and-a-half so yeah, that'll work."

Aria handed Melody a pair of brown leather high-heeled knee boots for her to put on.

"There. Now just do your make-up and you're done."

"Make-up? Do I look like I know how to do make-up?"

Aria hadn't thought of it. She never even noticed Melody didn't wear make-up. She was one of those rare beauties who was just naturally good-looking without any additives.

"Okay," she laughed. "I'll put a little eyeliner and lipstick on you. Not that you need it. Just to enhance what God already perfected."

"What God? There is no God." Melody spat, growing angry. Her entire demeanor had taken a turn for the worst in a mere split second.

"I can't believe you're saying that!" Aria fired back. "I know you've suffered a tragic loss, but you of all people should know the importance of faith. You used to be such a virtuous woman. Now look at you. You're obsessed with revenge, you swear like a sailor, and now you're sitting here telling me you no longer believe in God? How ungrateful can you be?"

"My daughter was sacrificed by a damn demon! Stabbed or cut open, I assume. Who knows? The bitch probably bathed in her blood. What the fuck do I have to be grateful for?"

"Your life maybe?" Aria answered with attitude. "You're still breathing, aren't you? You have a home, right? How about your family? Your mom and dad…aren't they still alive?"

"You know nothing about pain, Aria. You don't know what it's like to lose someone!"

"My mother is dying, if you haven't noticed! I'll admit I've been in denial about it, but every day I watch her slip further and further away and there's nothing I can do to stop it. Do you know how much that hurts? Tomorrow could be her last day….today could! I have no other family. She's all I have in this world. When she's gone I'll be completely alone and it breaks my heart watching her wither away to nothing. So don't tell me I don't know about pain!"

There was an uncomfortable silence in the room. Melody didn't know what to say. All she knew was her situation was nothing like Aria's.

"At least your mom has lived her life. My daughter never had a chance to."

"You should be glad your daughter was taken quickly instead of suffering a long, drawn out, slow, and painful death. As much as you'd like to pretend you don't, you know about faith, Melody. So have faith that what happened to your baby was God's plan. Everything happens for a reason and exactly when it's supposed to."

Melody absolutely hated when people said stuff like that. It didn't help or make her feel better one single bit. In fact it made her hate God more. She had always been a devout and by-the-book Christian. Her morals had been rock solid and she'd never strayed from her faith. God's plan involving the brutal sacrifice of her innocent baby girl was something she would never understand, never accept, and never, ever forgive Him for.

She wanted to curse Aria out using every four-letter word she had inducted into her vocabulary over the past three months. But they had something to accomplish and they needed to work together to do so. Melody knew she had to pick her battles and the potential cost of fighting this one was just not worth it.

"Okay, Aria," Melody said, deciding to let it go. "It's easy for you to be so faithful and optimistic while your mom is still alive. We'll see what you think about God later on."

VANNA B.

ChaPteR Six

Melody nervously walked into Laguardia Airport pulling a huge rolling suitcase behind her. She wished Aria was there to hold her hand but this mission was hers and hers alone. It was an important part of their plan. If she didn't pull this off, the entire thing would be ruined. She stood in the back of the long line of travelers waiting to walk through the metal detectors and have their bags and suitcases scanned in the X-ray machines. She spotted her target walking back and forth from station to station, ensuring everything was running smoothly. His face was serious and his posture was authoritative. The closer she got to the front of the line, the more nervous she became. Finally it was Melody's turn. She didn't know if she was much of an actress but she was about to find out.

She attempted to hoist her luggage onto the conveyor belt.

"Excuse me ma'am," a young female TSA worker said. "You're going to have to check that bag. It's too big for carry-on."

"What?" she asked. Are you sure? That can't be right. Can I speak with your manager, please?"

The young woman turned to summon her supervisor, but he was already making his way over

147

to see what the hold-up was. He was even taller up close and, to Melody's surprise, handsome. He was older than her by 20 years or so, but still he was an extremely attractive man. He had an exotic and ethnically ambiguous look – Melody couldn't figure out whether he was Hispanic, Middle Eastern, Mediterranean, or multiracial. All she knew was his bronze skin, thick eyebrows, and strong, masculine features were very much to her liking.

"Everything okay here?" he asked as he approached.

"Her bag," the girl said, pointing down to the large suitcase.

"I'm sorry, Miss, but that bag is too big to take onto the plane. You're going to have to check it."

"How do I do that?"

"Just take it back to the front counter where you checked in and they'll help you out."

"Checked in? I printed my ticket online so I thought I was already checked in. I'm sorry, this is my first time flying. Would you mind showing me where it is?"

Melody squeezed the supervisor's arm and flashed her pretty grin. He smiled back and nodded before offering to pull her bag for her.

"Wow, this is heavy. How'd a little lady like you handle this big old bag?"

"It's not the only big thing I've handled," she said suggestively.

His mind began to wander deep into the gutter as he eyed Melody's long, lean legs as she sashayed along in the short, tight skirt.

"What airline are you flying with, Miss…?"

"Jennifer," she said, filling in the gap he left open for her name. "My name's Jennifer. I'm flying with United."

"I'm Dean. Nice to meet you, Jennifer."

"Nice to meet you too, Dean."

"So it's your first time flying, you say? Where are you headed?"

"Um, Chicago. Visiting my aunt for a couple days."

"The Windy City, eh? I hear it's frigid there – even colder than it is here. I hope you packed some warm clothes."

"I sure did."

"Well, here we are. You just go up to that counter there and they'll get you checked in and take your bag."

"Thank you so much, Dean," said Melody looking into his eyes sincerely as she placed her hand on his chest. "You've been extremely helpful."

"My pleasure, Jennifer. It's not every day a supermodel walks through here, you know."

Melody giggled.

"I hope I'm not being too forward," Dean said, "but I was wondering if you might be single."

"Actually, I am," she smiled, hoping she didn't sound too eager. *Yes! Got him.* Her excitement bubbled up inside of her.

"How about you give me a call when you get back in town? I'd love to take you to dinner or something."

"I think that can be arranged."

Melody saved Dean's number in her phone and made sure he was out of sight before proceeding to exit the airport.

Chapter Seven

Melody breathed a big sigh of relief once she got back into the car with Aria.

"I'm glad that's over with. I'm not much of an actress."

"How did it go?"

"As well as can be expected. We're supposed to be going out to dinner when I 'get back in town' on Sunday," she said, fingering quotation marks in the air.

"That's great! I'm proud of you, girl."

"Thanks, but the hard part has yet to come. I still have to convince him and then there's dealing with Raven."

"Don't worry about Raven. We can kill her dead for good as long as we have the amulet. So just focus on that."

* * * * *

That night when Melody began tossing and turning in her sleep, Aria again slipped her arm over her body and held her close. As she squeezed tighter, Melody's movement gradually reduced to a tremble before stopping completely. She assumed Melody was now enjoying a peaceful slumber, until she heard her sob. Startled, Aria withdrew her arm.

"It's okay," Melody assured her. "You can hold me. It feels good. It felt good last night, too."

"I didn't know you knew. I thought you were sleeping," Aria said returning her arm to Melody's warm body. "I wasn't trying to violate you or anything. I just thought it would help you sleep better."

Melody turned under Aria's arm to face her. "It did."

In the midst of her tears Melody was able to offer her friend a sincere smile for her concern.

"The nightmares," Melody whispered, her face just inches from Aria's. "They seem so real. Every night they force me to experience the pain over again. It's so hard. And it hurts so bad."

Melody squeezed her eyes shut as if attempting to block out the horrific imagery. Aria used her thumb to wipe the tears from Melody's face, and then the strangest thing happened. Melody moved forward and placed the softest, sweetest kiss on Aria's lips. Aria was completely caught off guard. She found herself flustered; she didn't know what to say.

"I've seen the way you look at me," Melody explained. "Caught you staring more than a few times. Why didn't you just open your mouth and tell me you liked me?"

"I didn't want to make my houseguest uncomfortable. Plus, I didn't know you liked women."

"I don't," said Melody. "But I like you."

From there, Aria took the lead. She leaned into Melody, parting her wet lips with her tongue. She could tell it was Melody's first experience with a woman. Her body was tense and Aria could feel her heart pounding rapidly. Melody squeezed her thighs closed to try to stop her legs from trembling. She was nervous, but readily anticipating the experience to come.

"Just relax," Aria whispered into her ear before allowing her tongue to trail down to her collarbone. Melody untensed her body slightly as Aria kissed her neck and chest. She removed Melody's shirt and then her own. With sweat-moistened palms, Melody cupped Aria's breasts. Her nipples were already stiff. To Melody's surprise, Aria's quiet moans turned her on even more. She squirmed impatiently beneath her, pulling Aria closer. Aria ran her slender fingers across Melody's stomach as she tongued her breasts. She could feel the scar left where the baby was removed. It was the braille that told the story of the nightmare Melody had endured; the nightmare she relived every night as she slept. Aria kissed the scar tenderly. She wished she could kiss it away completely. But she was sure she could take her mind off of her bleak reality for at least a little while. Her hand moved further down south, rubbing Melody's sweet spot and prompting her to open her smooth, slim legs invitingly. Her juices had soaked through her white cotton panties. Aria skillfully removed them with her teeth then slowly kissed her way up from Melody's ankle to the inside of her thigh. She could feel Aria's warm breath sweep over her love box and she readily anticipated the feeling of her tongue on and in it. As her lips enveloped Melody's clitoris, her finger dipped into Melody's dripping hole. Aria loved the sound of Melody's moans. They were so soft and feminine, just like every inch of her body. She teased her pearl with stiff, slow licks. Melody wanted more. She grabbed the back of Aria's head and pulled her face closer. Aria, always eager to please, gave Melody exactly what she wanted. She unleashed what her ex-girlfriend called the Tornado Tongue, allowing it to encircle Melody's clit with a spiral motion as she expertly fingered her G-spot. Melody covered her head with the pillow to quiet her loudening moans. Aria continued to please her with quick tongue flicks up and down, pushing Melody to the verge of climax. She sucked her pearl and rubbed her G-spot with vigor. From beneath the pillow Melody yelled something incoherent before convulsing and coming so hard she squirted. Aria slurped up as much of her juices as she could, a satisfying reward for all her hard work.

Afterwards, Melody didn't say anything. She couldn't muster the energy to move. She just laid there in the dark next to Aria, confused. *Am I a lesbian?* she wondered. The only thing she knew for sure was that she wanted more. She was hooked.

ChaPteR Eight

Melody politely excused herself from the table of the French restaurant Dean had brought her to for their date. After using the bathroom and washing her hands she dialed Aria to update her on how her evening had gone thus far.

"So what's up?" Aria quickly answered her phone. "How's everything going?"

"Good!" Melody replied enthusiastically. "Better than expected, actually. We're at this posh French place. The food is excellent. He's really going the extra mile to impress me."

"Oh, well that's just wonderful," Aria stated dryly. "I'm glad you're having so much fun on your date."

"Relax, Aria...damn. You act like I'm here for recreation. I'm here because it's necessary, but since I have to be here what's wrong with me enjoying the food?"

"Nothing. Just making sure your head's still in the right place. Is he drinking?"

"Yeah, we've had a little champagne. Why?"

"That's not enough. He'll be easier to manipulate if he's intoxicated."

"Aria, please. He won't even remember what he's supposed to do if he's shitfaced when I tell him. Just let me handle this, okay? I'll be home afterwards."

Dinner with Dean turned out to be less of a chore than expected. The stern demeanor he exhibited while working was nowhere in sight. He proved to be a true gentleman and quite the entertaining date. He kept Melody laughing the whole time with his humorous stories of the things he'd seen in seven years of working at the airport. She spent much of the evening entranced by his deep, dark eyes.

After dinner they went back to his place. It was surprisingly neat and tidy. He gave Melody a brief tour of his apartment and showed her photos of his daughter who appeared to be only a few years younger than she was. It made her feel slightly uncomfortable for a moment until his strong hands on the small of her back quickly erased the discomfort. He took charge, pulling her slim body close to his. Dean slid his large hands across the soft, smooth skin of her back; first up and under her bra strap and then down into her panties, where he cupped her toned cheeks in his palms. He squeezed them so hard and it hurt so...good. Her pussy throbbed. It yearned to be touched and she could feel the moisture collecting between her legs. Dean grabbed the back of her neck and ran his fingers up through her sandy brown hair. He squeezed the handful of thick hair tightly in his fist, and Melody arched back, finding the pain quite pleasureful. The gentleman from the restaurant was gone. Dean had reverted back to the authoritative boss she'd witnessed at the airport. Melody loved his aggressiveness, and the way he was manhandling her was a major turn-on.

"Take your clothes off," he demanded sternly. His expression and voice told her he meant business. Melody found it sexy as hell; she quickly obliged, stripping down to her bra and thong. Next Dean removed his shirt and Melody took her first look at his ripped physique. It was obvious he worked out and took excellent care of his body. At forty he looked better than most of the young men her age, she thought.

"On your knees," Dean ordered.

Again she immediately obeyed, dropping to her knees as if worshipping him. She stared up into his austere eyes in anticipation of his next instructions.

Melody gulped down the large lump that had formed in her throat as Dean unbuckled his belt and pulled his zipper down. He kept his eyes on her the whole time, observing the effect he was having on her; her extreme nervousness was obvious. Inside her conflicted mind, Melody was tormented with a deep yearning for the very thing she feared. Darrin was the only man she'd ever been with and it was a horrible experience. She tried to recall Aria's comforting words, hoping to calm her jitters but before she could, Dean slapped his massive dick across her face. It was so big it actually hurt her cheek. Melody knew then there was no way she could have sex with him. She would not subject herself to the agony of him trying to ram that monster inside of her. She was going to have to make him cum orally. She just hoped she could do it; she'd never done it before. Lucky for her, Dean was all about dishing out orders.

"Lick it," he said. "Lick it like a popsicle."

She did as she was told, gliding her tongue up his pole as if she were trying to catch the melting drippings of her favorite treat, an orange creamsicle.

"Lick the head."

Her tongue slowly pirouetted around the tip of his hard cock, covering it in saliva.

"Gooood girl," he praised. "Now suck it."

Melody parted her lips and he inserted his penis into her mouth. As instructed, she closed her mouth around his rod and sucked, sliding her lips down as far as she could and then back up to the head.

"Grab it and jerk it."

She took the humongous meat stick into her hand and slowly stroked it up and down as she sucked harder. It was more difficult than she expected. Her fingers couldn't wrap all the way around its girth and she felt like her mouth was being stretched to the max. Melody realized there was a bit of coordination involved with such a task. Over and over she repeated the newly learned motion, gradually increasing her speed as she began to get the hang of it.

Dean pulled his pipe out of her mouth and smacked it back and forth across her face several times before sticking it back in. Melody was confused. She wasn't sure if it was intended to be some sort of punishment for doing a bad job or if it was just something he enjoyed doing.

Without warning, Dean grabbed the sides of her head with both his hands and shoved his dick down her throat. Melody thought she was going to choke on it but prevented it by laying her tongue flat and opening her mouth wider. Once Dean saw she could handle it like a big girl, he drilled her mouth, stroking her face like a rabid beast. Melody looked him straight in the eyes as he did, trying to get a read of whether she was doing any good. When he closed them shut and allowed his head to roll back Melody took that as good sign. It wasn't long before Dean pulled out of her throat and jerked his load onto her face. He painted her lips and chin with his cream then stood there smiling as he admired his work of art. Melody smiled back, happy that she had done well and discovered a new talent.

Dean was not finished with her yet. He hoped that was just the beginning.

"Take off your panties," he commanded.

Melody was a little scared to turn him down. She was afraid he'd get angry and that the whole plan would be botched. But despite her fear and regardless of how much he turned her on, she had to say no. She could not have intercourse with him.

"Um, Dean…I'm not ready yet. I'm a virgin," she lied. Even though physically it wasn't true, she would forever feel that she'd been unfairly cheated out of her first true sexual experience because of the fact that she'd been drugged and raped.

She studied him apprehensively, awaiting his response as he stared at her silently. She was relieved to see a genuine smile forming on his face.

"Really?" he asked. "That's actually kind of sweet." Dean went into the bathroom and came back with a washcloth. Instead of handing it to Melody, he gently wiped her mouth and chin, cleaning his semen off of her face. Melody assumed he was thinking of his daughter, and how he'd want her to be treated. But the only thing Dean was thinking about was the challenge that lied ahead of him. He knew there was no pussy better than virgin pussy. And the fact that it wouldn't be easy to get, made him want it even more.

Chapter Nine

Melody spent the night in Dean's arms as he dreamed about the moment he'd finally get a piece of her young, virgin ass. She didn't sleep much; instead she stayed up perfecting her script for the next morning. She knew exactly what she would say.

In the AM Dean pulled out all the stops. The breakfast in bed included homemade waffles, bacon, home fries, and scrambled eggs. A vase full of fresh cut flowers accompanied her plate on the wooden tray that he served up with a smile. Melody just assumed he was being sweet but, like her, Dean had an ulterior motive. He was determined to make Melody feel he was worthy of being her first.

After she had eaten, Dean took her tray to the kitchen and climbed back into bed beside her. He wondered what was wrong with her. For some reason she suddenly seemed melancholy.

"Everything okay?" he asked her.

"I'm fine," she sighed, unconvincingly.

"You sure? Seems like something's bothering you."

"Oh, it's nothing."

"Come on, baby. You can tell me. Maybe I can help somehow."

"I doubt it. It's just that my old roommate stole something very special to me; a necklace my grandmother had given me before she died. Today is the anniversary of her death so it's heavy on my mind."

"I'm sorry to hear that. Did you go to the police?"

"They had me file a report but they never did anything about it. They don't care about stuff like that. They have much bigger fish to fry in this city."

"That's a shame."

"I'm so sad. It's the only thing of hers that I had. All I want is to get it back. But there's nothing anyone can do unless…" She paused as if thinking before waving the idea off. "No, that's a stupid idea."

"Unless what? Tell me."

"No, it's silly. I wouldn't ask you to do something like that."

"What is it, Melody? If there's a way I can help you get your grandma's necklace back I'll do everything in my power to make it happen."

* * * * *

When Melody got back to Aria's apartment, Aria rushed her at the door.

"Oh my God! Where the hell have you been all night?"

"I decided to spend the night."

Aria grabbed Melody's hand and pulled her into the bedroom where they could talk privately.

"What the fuck, Mel?" yelled Aria. "That was not part of the plan. Why didn't you let me know? I was worried sick about you!"

"My phone was dead. I changed the plan up a little because I thought it would work out better, and it did. I'm sorry. I didn't consider you might worry."

"Why wouldn't I? You went out with some guy you don't even know and didn't come back. All types of crazy thoughts crossed my mind. He could have done something to you."

"Well I'm fine, okay? He's not a psycho or anything. He's just a regular guy. Chill out."

"Chill out? You like that motherfucker don't you?! What are you in love or something now?"

"What? Are you crazy?"

"I thought this was business. I didn't know you were the type to mix business with pleasure."

"I'm not! I can't believe you're acting so fucking jealous! I did what I had to do to make shit work."

"I should've known your hetero ass wouldn't be able to sleep with a man without getting all emotionally attached."

"I didn't even have sex with him! You are tripping right now, Aria. Let me know when you calm down and get it together."

Melody turned to leave but Aria rushed past her out the bedroom door and through the living

163

room. She grabbed her coat and was preparing to exit the apartment.

"What are you doing? It's your place," Melody said, following behind her, "You stay. I'll leave."

Aria yanked the door open and they both froze when they saw who was standing outside the door.   It   was   Darrin.

CHAPTER TEN

Darrin charged into the apartment with a butcher's axe held high. Melody instinctively ran while Aria stood her ground to fight. Aria's mother was awakened by all the commotion and started trying to crawl out of bed when she saw an axe-wielding intruder in their home attacking her daughter. Darrin swung the axe twice, missing Aria's throat by inches both times. He swung it a third and this time Aria was able to catch his arm in mid swing. She struggled to twist his wrist, attempting to loosen his grip on the weapon. Darrin persisted, though, and held steady as he pushed harder on the axe that was now just centimeters from her face. Aria dodged, quickly bobbing her head to the side just as Darrin gave a final thrust that would have drove the axe right through her nose and split her face in half. She grunted loudly as she slammed her forehead into his and watched the head-butt send him flying back holding his aching dome. Aria took advantage of him being momentarily distracted by the pain and kicked the axe out of his hand. But Darrin had a back-up plan that he pulled from his boot – a black revolver. He aimed the gun at Aria and pulled the trigger at the same instance that Melody leapt from the kitchen and stabbed him in the back with a carving knife.

The gun went off but the bullet missed Aria. Darrin yelled out as the pain shot through him, never losing his grip on the revolver's handle. He spun around, aiming the gun at Melody. Before he could fire it, Aria kicked the handle of the knife still stuck in his back, pushing the blade all the way in. Darrin dropped the gun and fell to the floor screaming as blood gushed from his wound. That is when Aria noticed her mother's movement had stopped. With a heavy feeling in the pit of her stomach, her eyes shot across the living room to her mom's bed. There she lied, eyes frozen open in horror with an oozing bullet hole in the side of her head.

"Mom! Noooo!" Aria yelled as she and Melody ran to her bedside. They never even realized the bullet intended for Aria had struck her mother. Melody dialed 9-1-1 as Aria attempted to induce a response from her mom.

"Come on, Mom, wake up!" she cried as she desperately shook her mother's body despite the fact that she obviously was dead. Melody cried silent tears as she watched the tragic scene. She was hurting so badly for Aria, but she knew from her own loss that no amount of words or affection would help. Just as she wanted to avenge her daughter's death, Aria would want to avenge her mother's, Melody thought. She picked Darrin's gun up from the floor and rushed out the door. She followed the trail of blood all the way to the end of the hall and down the stairs to the street. The trail ended at the curb where Darrin had stepped into the taxi that took him to the hospital.

The remainder of the night was long and bleak. It consisted of an apartment full of police, nonstop tears, and answering the same questions over and over again. Melody did her best to comfort Aria and support her through the process. The worst part was when they had to take her mother's body away. Aria did not want to let go. It took six officers to pry her away from the corpse. Witnessing the whole ordeal made Melody realize that what Aria had said about her being lucky was the truth. She did feel that she was sort of lucky to have never seen her daughter's dead body. There was no grotesque, morbid image of a mutilated infant corpse embedded in her mind. The only way she saw her daughter was as she imagined her: beautiful and angelic.

She and Aria were both glad when the police had finally gone. Aria cried herself to sleep and, just as she had done for her, Melody was there to hold Aria the whole night through.

VANNA B.

Chapter Eleven

Dean kept his eyes peeled for a uniquely dressed young woman with bright red hair. She wasn't hard to spot at all and he almost had to pick his jaw up from the floor when he saw her. "Jennifer" had failed to mention that her "ex-roommate" was an exotic beauty with a body that was out of this world.

"Take five," he instructed the employee working the station Raven was approaching. "Go and get yourself a soda or something."

"Thanks, boss!" The young man eagerly obliged.

Dean watched Raven lift her bag and place it onto the conveyor belt. When Raven slid out of her coat Dean's dick stiffened at the sight of her full breasts popping out of her shirt. Her pants were extremely tight; he could see the plumpness of her pussy lips right through them. Dean ogled her body as she switched her curvy hips straight through the metal detector. It beeped.

"Miss, would you please remove all metal objects and place them in one of those bins?"

Annoyed, Raven huffed while taking off her silver bangles and spiked earrings.

"The necklace too, please," he prompted.

"Seriously?" She clutched the amulet to her chest, not wanting to remove it.

"I'm sorry sweetie, but rules are rules. I can't let you through here until this machine stops beeping. You have to take off anything metal. It's just going right through this machine and afterwards you can put it back on. I promise nothing will happen to it."

"Whatever." She rolled her eyes and reluctantly removed the amulet and placed it into a plastic bin. She watched the conveyor belt roll it into the X-ray scanner as she walked through the metal detector. Again, it beeped.

"Fuck!"

"Relax, hon. It's probably just the rings in your facial piercings."

"Yeah, well guess what…I got piercings in my nipples and one in my clit, too. I know you don't expect me to take all of them out. If you make me miss my fucking flight, you asshole, I swear…"

By now the other employees were watching to see how Dean planned to handle the disrespectful woman. He never let anyone talk to him the way Raven was but, in fact, it was turning him on ridiculously. His pipe jumped with every octave her voice raised.

"I'll tell you what; how about I just frisk you to make sure you're not hiding any contraband on you."

"Where the fuck would I hide it? Look how tight my goddamn clothes are."

"Well, if you'd prefer I just take you in the back and strip search you…"

"You'd just love that, wouldn't you? I see your dick getting hard right now just thinking about it."

Dean smiled and shrugged. It was true. In his mind he had already bent her sexy ass over the table and fucked her brains out. Nothing would have pleased him more than watching her strip down to her birthday suit and trying to convince her to let him slide up inside her. Hell, as horny as he'd gotten just by looking at her, he would have gladly paid her for sex.

"Just do what you have to do and hurry it the fuck up."

"Okay, sweetie. Let's get you your jewelry first."

The plastic bin containing Raven's things was just about to roll out of the X-ray machine. Dean reached inside and allowed the replica amulet to slip out of his sleeve and into the bin. Then he took the real one into his hand and closed his fist around it before picking up the bin.

"Here you go, dear."

Raven snatched the bin and Dean slid the amulet into his pocket while she secured the phony around her neck. Then came the moment Dean was waiting for.

Raven spread her legs and extended her arms to the side to allow Dean to pat her down. He felt the tops and bottoms of her arms before cupping up under her breasts. The heavy mounds rose and then dropped once he removed his hands. Watching them jiggle made his cock begin to rise even more. He patted down her back, then ran his hands down her sides very slowly, taking the time to feel every inch of her sharp curves. With a smirk plastered on her face, Raven stared into his eyes fully aware of the erection in his pants. His gaze remained fixated on hers as he dropped down to place his hands on one of her ankles. Moving slowly to enjoy every second of it, he allowed his hands to slide up her leg to the top of her thick thigh. Just to toy with him, Raven ran her tongue across her top lip then bit down on the bottom one seductively. Again, Dean squatted down, placing his hands on her other ankle. He locked his eyes right between her legs on the imprint of her labia. She was soaked. Her juices had seeped through the fabric of her clothing and Dean swore he could see her vagina pulsating right through her pants. His hands began to tremble as they continued roaming up her thigh. Further and further they crept and when his fingers landed at her moisture-saturated center, she let out the softest little moan. No one else could hear it but Dean did. He erupted right then and there, stumbling and almost falling over as his semen soaked through his boxers and leaked down his leg.

As Dean hurried off, Raven picked up her bag and strutted toward her gate.

"Men," she chuckled to herself. "So, so weak."

Chapter Twelve

The day after the death of Aria's mother was spent in mourning. Aria stayed in bed and Melody did her best to care for her. She remained by her side, consoled her, and prepared all her meals while Aria grieved her loss.

On the second day they slept late into the afternoon. Aria awoke in the arms of a still-sleeping Melody. Just like on the previous day, her first instinct was to go into the kitchen to make her mother breakfast. Then she remembered she was gone. Aria didn't suffer from claustrophobia but at that moment she felt the same way claustrophobics feel in tight spaces. She felt as if the walls were caving in on her as she was overcome with the unbearable grief all over again. She threw Melody's arm off of her as she gasped for breath. When she had finally started breathing normally, she no longer felt the urge to get up, or even to move. She just lied there, trembling and crying.

Melody was awakened by the sound of Aria weeping beside her. Today was the day they had been planning for; the day when they'd finally give Raven the death she deserved. But Aria was obviously in no condition to do much of anything. Her mother's death had her an emotional wreck and Melody understood that she might not be up to it.

She knew facing Raven alone was a bad idea, but she had come too far and sacrificed too much to turn back now. If Aria wasn't going to come with her, she would just have to do it solo.

Aria soon felt Melody's arms tightening around her body once again, and her soft voice attempting to comfort and soothe her.

"I'm here for you, Aria. I'm here."

Melody knew better than to tell her it was going to be okay. It would never be okay. Her mother was dead and she was not coming back. There was nothing okay about it. She just wanted Aria to know that she was there for her and she wasn't going anywhere.

"Mel?" Aria managed to sob.

"Yeah?"

"You know what I said before – that I'd be completely alone when my mom dies?"

"Yeah."

"Well, it's not true. I've got you."

"Yes, you do, Aria. You got me. And I'm not alone either because I have you. I'm here for you. And I'm going to stay right here by your side."

Melody squeezed her tightly and this time Aria embraced her back. The two women shared a long, loving embrace.

"I love you, Aria," Melody said. She hadn't even thought twice about the words before they rolled off her tongue. There was nothing to think about. They came straight from her heart and saying them felt as natural as breathing. She was in love and she knew it was for real.

"I love you too," Aria whispered back.

One by one, Melody kissed the teardrops on Aria's face, until they were all gone. Aria pressed her lips to Melody's and could taste her own salty tears. She was mourning and miserable. Melody understood that better than anyone, but at the same time she wondered how long it would be until Aria regained her usual vibrancy and luster. She already missed Aria's smile and couldn't wait to see it again. She wished she could say or do something to perk her up. She thought Aria deserved to feel good, even if it was just for a moment.

"I want to taste you," Melody whispered into Aria's ear as her hands roamed up her shirt to her braless breasts. Aria shuddered at the feeling of Melody's cool palms on her warm skin. She turned into her, welcoming her touch and inviting her to proceed. Melody obliged by sliding her hand into Aria's panties and dipping a finger into her honeypot. Aria was eager and moist. There was no turning back now. Melody nervously moved Aria's underwear to one side as she allowed her tongue to become acquainted with her flower. She began with long, slow licks, allowing every part of her tongue to make contact with Aria's pulsating pearl. She wasn't sure exactly what she was doing but the way Aria writhed about was an indication that she did not want her to stop. She sucked her clit as if she was trying to suck the pain right out of her body.

She licked her kitty softly. And as she continued pleasing Aria, she simultaneously tended to her own needs below. She squeezed her clit between her thumb and index finger while her middle and ring fingers plunged in and out of her dripping pussy. Aria threw back the covers and quickly slid her panties off, flinging them across the room. She then removed Melody's as well as pushed her down onto the bed. Melody looked on in confusion as Aria straddled her widespread legs and lowered her vagina onto hers. She almost burst out laughing at the squishy sounds their genitals made as they rubbed against one another like two animals in heat. But the silly smile soon left her face and was replaced by a look of sheer pleasure. She had no idea it would feel so phenomenal. Aria continued to dominate the experience, which Melody didn't mind at all. She dictated the pace and controlled the rhythm. Aria grabbed Melody's neck and kissed her wet lips. Their hands explored one another's bodies as their tongues mingled, and they soon climaxed in unison, exchanging saliva and sexual juices.

The orgasm must have done Aria some good, because afterwards she didn't revert back to her previous state of grief. Instead, she seemed focused on what lie ahead of them.

"The bitch is going down tonight," she announced. "Today will be the end of Raven."

Melody looked at Aria with uncertainty. "You mean you're gonna do it with me?"

"Yeah. We're in this thing together now." Aria took Melody's hand into hers and their fingers intertwined.

"You sure you're up to it?" Melody asked.

"Absolutely. I can't let you go at her alone. I'm not going to lose you too. Besides, she has it coming. She was the reason my mom was bedridden in the first place. As far as I'm concerned, Raven is the reason she's dead. She has to die…today," she reiterated firmly. After a couple more minutes she rose from the bed with determination. "Let's do this."

Their day was spent in preparation, going over their plans and running through different scenarios that could possible play out. There was no room for error when dealing with a being as dangerous as Raven; the slightest mistake could be deadly. Luckily, they already had one egg in their basket. Melody smiled as she held up the dangling amulet and watched it swing back and forth on its chain. Her eyes sparkled with excitement. It was almost time and she could not wait.

VANNA B.

Chapter Thirteen

"Where the hell is she?" Aria was growing antsy waiting for Raven to exit the airport.

"Just be patient," Melody said. "She's gotta come out through here. Her bags are coming to this baggage claim area."

"That rationale makes no sense whatsoever. She could have easily gone through any other exit after getting her luggage."

"Come on, Aria. Why the fuck would she go out of her way to go out another door when there's one right here? Just shut up and wait. Damn…" Aria's attitude was really starting to annoy Melody.

"Well, look…it's 1 AM. Her flight was scheduled to land almost two hours ago."

"Maybe it was delayed. Her bag could've gotten held up. Anything could've happened."

"Maybe your little boyfriend just purposely gave you the wrong information because he didn't get any pussy."

"Oh please," Melody scoffed. "You don't know the first thing about men."

"I know they don't like when you don't give up the vag."

"Well, whatever. The info is straight. Have some patience."

As soon as the words left her lips, Raven walked through the sliding doors. Melody shot Aria a look that said "I told you so" and pulled down the brim of her baseball cap in preparation. This was the moment she'd been waiting for. Aria threw the hood of her jacket over her head and the women proceeded in Raven's direction cautiously. They watched her step into a taxi before hailing their own and ordering it to follow Raven's. Their driver did a good job of keeping up with the other taxi, and a twenty-minute ride later, Raven's cab stopped in the heart of Hell's Kitchen and she exited the vehicle.

Aria and Melody paid their driver and watched Raven descend the stairs into the subway.

"We can't lose her," Melody said, keeping her eyes locked on Raven's cherry-hued coiffure as they followed her through the crowds of travelers pouring out of the A train doors.

Raven walked to the end of the platform and jumped down onto the tracks, disappearing into the dark tunnel.

"Where's she going?" Melody was starting to worry.

"Her new lair must be down here. These subway tunnels are full of vile creatures. It's dark and cold – just how they like it – and they know they can stay relatively secluded."

"Big downgrade from the defiled church."

"Yeah, consider that a mansion and down here the projects."

Aria lowered herself onto the tracks before helping Melody. Once they were both safely down, she handed Melody a glass dagger. Like her arrows, it was filled with holy water and was lethal to any unsanctified being. They began stalking Raven up the tunnel, being careful to follow at a safe distance so as not to be seen or heard by her. The element of surprise would give them an advantage over her if they could manage a sneak attack. As they moved closer to Raven, Aria took an arrow and placed it into the bow. She drew it back slowly while perfecting her aim and then gently released her grip, letting the arrow rip. As it hurled toward Raven she vanished into thin air.

"Shit!" Aria exclaimed.

Raven quickly removed the amulet from around her neck, unaware that the real one had been swapped for a phony. The sound of her sinister laugh echoed through the tunnel.

Aria and Raven carefully surveyed their surroundings in search of her. With their backs up against one another's, they continued scanning the area. Melody's heart raced as she held the dagger tightly. Aria retrieved another arrow. Carefully placing the holy water-filled vial on the nock, she pulled back the bowstring, preparing to release the arrow as soon as Raven reappeared. Their eyes circled the underground space as they silently anticipated the moment she'd attack.

The ground began to tremble beneath their feet. From a distance, they could hear the rumbling of a train making its way toward them.

"Maybe she's gone," whispered Melody.

"No," Aria assured her. "I can smell her filthy, evil scent."

"Yeah? Well I smell, pussy!" Melody yelled into the air, her voice resounding all around them. "That bitch Raven ain't so tough, after all!"

"What are you doing?" Aria asked in a hushed tone, eyes bulging in bewilderment. Melody knew exactly what she was doing, and soon Aria would, too.

"Some succubus she is," Melody continued. "Hiding like a little bitch! We're right here. Are you too scared to face us?" Melody screamed with outstretched arms as she walked further into the tunnel, leaving Aria behind. "I can't believe it. You're petrified, aren't you, Raven? A true coward!"

"Melody...stop!" Aria walked after Melody. She knew Raven was more than capable of killing an untrained individual like Melody in the blink of an eye, and she feared that is exactly what would happen if she continued to anger and provoke her. If she caught Melody alone, the outcome could be lethal. But still Melody continued.

"Show yourself!" she demanded. "Why are you so afraid to come out? I know why. Because you're nothing but a pussy! You're real tough acting but get weak men to do your dirty work for you. You'll kill an innocent baby but you won't dare show your face right here right now because you're pussy! 100 percent, Grade-A, certified PUSSY!"

"We'll see about that!" Raven growled from above.

Their necks craned up to the ceiling over Melody where Raven's eyes were glowing an intense red as she hung upside down. Aria knew this meant trouble. Raven's eyes only glowed on rare occasions when she was really furious.

"Shit!" she yelled, steadying her aim. "Mel, run!"

Raven sprang at Melody like a striking cobra. She managed to dodge out of her way just in the nick of time. Raven landed on the tracks and flew after Melody, pursuing her as she darted through the dark subway tunnel. By now the rumble of the incoming train had grown into a roar; the ground quaked as the train approached the station. Straight ahead, Melody was facing the blinding headlight of a speeding 430-ton train. And fast on her heels was a bloodthirsty demon from the pits of Hell. Aria yelled out to Melody but the train's blaring horn drowned her voice out completely. Melody had to make a move fast or she'd be mangled by the incoming train. Finally she dove off the tracks and rolled into the wall, breaking the glass dagger in the process.

As the train continued by, a now weaponless Melody looked to her left and right in search of

Raven, but she didn't see her on either side. She glanced up over her head and Raven was not there either. When the final car of the train zipped by, there she was, hovering on the other side of the track, glaring at Melody with her eyes still aglow, and twirling 15 feet of heavy duty steel towing chain above her head like a lasso. Before Melody even had a chance to flea, Raven slung the thick chain across the track. It swung around Melody's neck multiple times, wrapping tightly.

"Eh, this one's too skinny! Should I throw it back?" Raven joked as she slowly reeled in the chain, dragging Melody across to her. She failed to notice Aria creeping behind her.

Or at least she pretended to. Aria sent an arrow whisking through the air aimed directly at the back of Raven's head. But at the last second Raven dodged, leaving the arrowhead to skim the surface of Melody's scalp, parting it straight down the middle before lodging into the graffiti-covered wall behind her.

"Close one," said Raven, smiling diabolically, "but almost doesn't count." The other end of the chain whipped around, striking Aria across the face before swinging back and wrapping around the length of her body, rendering her arms and legs useless.

Dragging Melody along like a dog on a leash, Raven leapt over to Aria. Raven repeatedly yanked both ends of the chain, drawing the women closer and closer together. The chain tightened around Melody's neck, restricting her airway, and, at the same time, squeezed Aria's body so tightly her lungs became unable to expand. They now stood face to face struggling to breathe as they looked into each other's eyes for the last time.

So this is it, thought Melody to herself. *This is how it ends.* At last she realized how truly foolish she was to think she could eliminate a being as evil as Raven; a force that proved to be stronger than even Aria. Her judgment had been clouded by hatred. She was so bent on revenge she signed her own death certificate in pursuit of it. She had no regrets about her decisions, though. In her last moments she thought about her daughter. She closed her eyes, giving in to the darkness as she prepared to see her baby for the first time ever. Staring into one another's fear-filled eyes, Melody and Aria exchanged silent goodbyes. Melody leaned closer to nestle her face into Aria's neck. It was the closest they would get to a hug; she wanted to touch Aria one final time.

"Awww, how sweet," Raven sneered. "You two get to die together."

With her last bit of remaining energy Melody thrust forward and bit down onto one of the arrowheads sticking out of the leather quiver on Aria's back. Her mouth stung from the multiple cuts inflicted by the tiny shards of glass as it shattered into pieces. She spit the mouthful of holy water and glass directly into Raven's face.

"Ahhhhhh!" The deafening shriek echoed throughout the tunnel as the blessed water singed her face, burning right through her skin like acid. As soon as Raven released her hold on the chain to grab her face, it loosened from around their bodies, allowing them to breathe again. Melody immediately grabbed another arrow and drove it right into Raven's forehead.

"You can't kill me! I'll be back and this time I'm going to destroy you both!" Raven screamed as the holy water was dispersed throughout her brain.

"No, you won't," sang Melody, dangling the amulet in front of her face. As Raven reached out to grab it, Melody slammed it to the ground with all her might.

"Noooooo!" Raven scrambled after it but it was too late. As soon as the black jewel hit the floor it exploded into a huge ball of fire. And so did Raven. The holy water had finally made its way down to her heart, burning through it and causing her body to erupt into flames.

Melody and Aria stood staring in amazement at the burning fire. They were in awe. It didn't quite seem real.

"That's it...she's gone," said Aria. Melody was silent. Aria turned to her and could see the reflection of the dancing flames in her glassy eyes as she continued watching the fire burn. Raven was dead and she was the one who had killed her. It still seemed surreal to her.

"She's really dead," Melody finally said.

"Yeah, so I guess your mission is complete."

"Not quite. I still have one more loose end to tie up."

VANNA B.

Chapter Fourteen

Aria and Melody found Darrin's apartment in disarray when they startled him by kicking his door in. He had a trash bag in his hand and appeared to be in the midst of packing. They coolly strutted in as if they'd been invited while Darrin stood frozen, confused by their intrusion.

"You going somewhere?" Aria asked, looking around the cluttered apartment.

Darrin's eyes shifted nervously. He was so weak there was no way he could possibly fight or run.

"Relax, man. We're not here to fight. We actually came with a peace offering," said Melody.

Darrin prayed it was true. With his back bandaged up from their recent altercation, he was in no condition to do much of anything. He wasn't even supposed to have left the hospital yet, but he had hoped to grab a few of his things and vacate the apartment before he received a visit from Aria and Melody, who had become more than a thorn in his ass. So much for that.

Darrin kept his guard up as he eyed the women suspiciously. He knew better than to trust them. Hell, it hadn't even been 72 hours since he attacked them in Aria's home and had Melody plunge a knife into his back. Something was up.

Melody stretched her arm out, presenting a plastic Duane Reade shopping bag.

"I feel bad about all that's happened, Darrin," Melody said sympathetically. "I really didn't mean to hurt you last night, but I didn't know how else to get you to stop. You were about to kill Aria. I know that your actions weren't completely your fault. You were a victim too. Raven had you under her spell. I'm getting ready to go back to Chicago for good, but before I leave I just wanted to do the God-like thing and forgive you."

Her eyes were kind and honest as she spoke. She no longer looked like the jaded, revenge-driven woman she had recently become. She just looked like the regular old Melody that Darrin knew and used to love. Still, Darrin didn't trust her. He looked down at the bag she was offering him, wondering what it could possibly contain.

"Throw it over," he demanded suspiciously.

Melody tossed the bag across to him and it landed at his feet with a thud. Whatever was in it sounded pretty heavy. Darrin carefully opened it and peeked inside. Melody and Aria smirked at each other in anticipation of his reaction to its contents and that is when he saw it.

Darrin shrieked in horror and dropped the bag as he fearfully backed away. The shrill pitch of his scream made it sound like it came from a teenage girl instead of a grown man. Raven's bloody severed head rolled out of the bag and across the floor to where Aria and Melody were standing. Melody took a final look at the petrified expression on what was left of Raven's evil face before drop kicking the head and sending it hurling full-speed at Darrin with its stringy red hair flying behind it. His anguished screams continued as he stumbled backwards and fell into a large cardboard box. Aria and Melody could not stop laughing as Melody approached the box and positioned her gun at Darrin's temple.

"Now you two can spend the rest of eternity together in Hell."

A sick smile spread across Darrin's lips. He nodded his head as he repeated, "Yes, together forever...yeah." Melody looked into Darrin's glazed eyes, which confirmed what she already knew: Darrin was long gone. Raven had killed him and turned him into a monster like her. Still, it would bring Melody much satisfaction to know he would no longer be walking the earth.

The thought of spending eternity with Raven eased Darrin's deranged mind until the hollow point bullet tore through his skull and sent his brains out the other side of his head.

Pulling the trigger felt as good as Melody had imagined. It was liberating in a way, and made her feel like she had truly completed her mission and had now written a satisfying end to this horrifying chapter of her life story.

"What now?" Aria asked, as they strolled out of the apartment and back onto the chilly Brooklyn streets.

"I don't know. I guess I never really thought about what I'd do once it was all over. I didn't plan anything beyond the plans that were just carried out."

"Stay in New York with me," Aria said. She didn't know what she'd do without Melody, especially now that her mother was gone. "You could finish your degree. I think you'd make a pretty damn good demon hunter too, now that you've got some experience under your belt."

"Nah," Melody said coldly, staring out at the vast urban jungle before them. "I don't think so."

Aria's smile vanished. Sadness and disappointment consumed her as she realized everything Melody had said that morning was just mere pillow talk. She had told her what she wanted to hear only to motivate her enough to complete their mission...and that was all it was. Now that it was over, it was only natural that their relationship be over too. Aria cursed herself for being blinded by love. *Should have seen it coming*, she thought.

"Sorry," Melody said remorselessly. "I can't stick around here and be fighting demons and shit, Aria. That's your thing. That's not me."

"I understand," Aria replied in a sullen tone.

"Now a demon hunter's wife?" she perked up. "That I can do."

Aria's eyes rose from the sidewalk to meet Melody's mischievous gaze and her face lit up with joy. The two of them burst into laughter as Melody jumped back, dodging Aria's incoming playful punches. When Aria caught her lady she pulled her in close and they embraced one another lovingly under the streetlight just as the sun began to rise at the dawn of a new day.

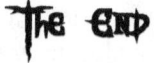

Thank you for reading *The Succubus*!

If you enjoyed this book, please leave a review for it on Amazon and tell a friend about it. Be sure to check out my other titles, *Fancy*, *Fancy 2*, and *Knock-off Nina*.

You can connect with me on social networks and subscribe to my newsletter, as well as the Hope Street Publishing newsletter, via the web addresses below.

<u>Connect with Vanna B.</u>

www.HopeStreetPublishing.com
Facebook: Author Vanna B
Instagram: VannaB215
Twitter: @MsVannaB

About the Author

Vanna B. is an author and publisher of fiction novels. The Hope Street Publishing CEO is a native of Philadelphia, PA and received her BA in journalism from Temple University. Writing has been a life-long passion of hers and she always planned on authoring books.

Vanna's professional writing career began with newspapers and magazines, where she served as a restaurant reviewer, proofreader, advice columnist and staff writer covering a range of topics including current events, local politics and culture. After making the decision to leave the workforce to stay home to raise her son, she began penning her first novel, *Fancy*.

Fancy went on to be a huge success, landing on the Amazon Kindle best-sellers list for multiple categories, earning Vanna the 2012 Philly Hip Hop award for "Best Author," being featured in *The Source Magazine*, and receiving overwhelmingly positively reviews. This year its sequel, *Fancy 2*, and her novel, *Knock-off Nina*, also made the Kindle best-sellers list, and Vanna was nominated for two AAMBC Awards as well as two Urban Literary Awards.

"I'm incredibly grateful that my work is being so well received," Vanna says. "I love writing and sharing my gift with others, and I work very hard at providing top-notch material with the goal of bringing readers a unique and memorable experience."

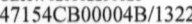